The Octagonal Room

The Octagonal Room

by

Patricia Brandt

ISBN: 1-58961-418-6

Published by PageFree Publishing, Inc.
109 South Farmer Street
Otsego, MI 49078
(269) 692-3926
www.pagefreepublishing.com

To my children; Marcia, Paige and Drew. Without them, I would be void of inspiration. Thank you to Mark Barocco of Renaissance Conservatories and to Dorothy Hamilton for allowing me to use the image of the spectacular octagonal room on the cover.

ONE

Nancy

I told you before that I am not going to eat this shit." Bob violently threw the half full jar of mayonnaise into the plastic kitchen wastebasket. The sound of the breaking glass made Nancy flinch. "How many times do I have to tell you that I hate that brand? I never want to see this crap in my fridge again. What do I have to do to get it through your thick head?"

Nancy clenched her teeth, took a deep breath and made a conscious effort not to show emotion. She knew from past experiences that showing fear only heightened his rage. "I'll go to the store later and buy a different brand." It was barely noticeable that her hand trembled as she turned the page of the morning newspaper.

It would take about twenty minutes before Nancy would find herself, predictably, in the bathroom. She hoped that he would be gone when she made her trip to the toilet bowl. She didn't want him to know that he was the victor.

"What kind of idiot would ever plan a reunion on a Sunday, stupidest thing I ever heard." He paused a moment to study the expression on his wife's face. The corners of his lips turned up before he continued. "That cheap ass class of yours probably did it to save a couple of bucks. But in spite of it, I can't say it was a total write off. I think I have George Pearson convinced to give me the policy on his farm. No thanks to you. What in hell were you thinking? You sat in the corner with that whore friend of yours and that snobby bitch from Chicago. Thank God, twenty-five year class reunions only come once, or you would be going to the next one alone."

It always amazed Nancy how Bob's personality did a complete turn around when he talked with his insurance clients. In her mind, Nancy referred to this transformation as his Jeckel and Hyde mode. She always thought of him as two men, the one in private and the one he displayed to everybody else. But it was only in her mind, never daring to tell him to his face, even in her wildest dreams.

She said nothing for a moment, trying to phrase her comment so not to infuriate her husband. Her voice took on a low tone. "I wish you would give Melissa and Eden a chance, I think...."

"No, you don't think. You never think, Nancy. You always seem to forget that I have a reputation that I need to maintain in this town. I forbid you to be cavorting with those two, especially Melissa Perkins."

Her lips quivered and her eyes lowered. "Bob, I hope what I'm going to say isn't going to upset you. Eden asked Melissa and me to spend Friday night at her home in Oak Park. We're going to go shopping downtown and eat in a fancy restaurant on Saturday. It's this coming weekend. So, please don't give me any problems. I really want to go."

"No."

"Is that all you have to say, no?" Nancy nervously slicked back the dishwater brown hair from her face. She wore no make-up other than light lip-gloss. Bob hated her to wear make-up. She averted her eyes, unable to look at her husband directly.

"It's the only answer you deserve. You're not going. Simple is all you seem to understand and you don't even seem to understand that very well." Bob pulled out the chair at their small kitchen table and sat, his eyes bold, never diverted from Nancy's face. The kitchen, in keeping with the style of the house was decorated in country colonial, tasteful, but bland.

"Hello, you two." Bob's mother, Doris, walked through the back kitchen door. How Nancy hated that she never knocked. She always thought it was an overt sign of disrespect. Bob shot his wife a stern look as a warning not to continue their discussion in the presence of his mother. "I was hoping that I'd catch you at home."

Doris was a large boned woman in her late sixties, definitely enjoying her make-up and jewelry. Today she sported big, gaudy, jeweled earrings. Her gray hair was bleached blond, permed, and stiffly lacquered. Nancy could not help but smile when she thought of something that Melissa once said. Doris wore her short hair straight in the back and curled on the top. Melissa referred to it as the buffalo do.

Bob stood and gave his mother an affectionate kiss on her heavily painted cheek. Doris's perfume was so strong that the floral scent could be smelled long after she left the room. If Bob wasn't around, Nancy sprayed air freshener and opened the windows when she left, even in the winter. What if Doris, who liked to think of herself as Rockton's society matron, knew that her perfume virtually turned Nancy's stomach?

Nancy instinctively walked to the coffee pot, as he did every other time Doris reared her ugly head "Please, dear, not coffee. I would prefer a cup of tea if you don't mind. It'll give you a chance to use that darling teapot that I gave you. Nancy, I will need you to drive me to Rockford on Saturday. I got some good coupons in the mail for Bartlett's, half off. I need some new table linens, and you know how I hate to drive into the city. I'll even treat to lunch."

"Doris, I would hardly call Rockford, the city. You know, I would be happy to drive you, but not this weekend. I was just telling Bob that I'm going to spend Friday and Saturday in Chicago with Eden McNeal and Melissa Perkins."

Bob painfully squeezed Nancy's shoulder in an attempt to silence her. "Nancy will be more than glad to drive you to Rockford on Saturday morning, Mother."

He managed to produce a fake smile, solely for his mother's benefit.

"Melissa Perkins? I would never have dreamed that you would associate with somebody like her. You have to be careful, dear, Bob has his business reputation to maintain."

Nancy's eyes were downcast as she looked intently into the cup of black coffee that she pretended to enjoy. She was not going to give in to the depression that was looming, waiting for her to accept so it could bore into her head. "I've known Melissa since kindergarten. She is a good person with a heart of gold. She would give you the shirt off her back."

Bob quickly interrupted. "Rumor has it that she's given lots of guys the shirt off her back."

Nancy keenly listened, but knew, too well, that there was not winning once Bob and his mother ganged up on her. History proved that she always folded under. "Bob, who are we to judge anybody? Melissa has never deliberately hurt anybody. In fact, she has even stayed friends with her ex husbands. I don't think that I want to discuss this any further."

"Good, no more discussion. Mother, like I said, Nancy will be delighted to take you to Rockford on Saturday." He quickly stood in an attempt to finalize his last statement.

Nancy's heart palpated as she felt the bile rise in her throat. But somehow, this morning felt different. She was on the verge of snapping. It took many years of marriage before Queen Doris accepted her. Even now, Nancy was not sure if she was accepted or just used.

"I'll let you ladies work out your plans for Saturday. I can't waste anymore time here. I need to get to the office." Bob grabbed a white folder laid on the counter before he exited. He didn't miss a chance to give Nancy a look with narrowed eyes before closing the door.

There was an uncomfortable silence. Finally, Nancy spoke. "Doris, I don't mean to be rude or disagreeable. But, Bob and I have only been separated when he's been at insurance conferences out of state. I need this time, and I believe that I deserve it. I don't expect you to talk to Bob on my behalf. I guess that I'll need to take care of it."

Doris took a long sip of her now tepid tea, which consisted of a cup with a tea bag, not the pot of tea that she expected. She looked coyly at her daughter-in-law. "Of course, I am not going to intervene because I don't agree with you. This trip is a bad idea. Poor Bob has been under a lot of stress at the agency and I don't think you should aggravate him."

Nancy shocked herself at her own boldness. "Aggravate him? What about me? I never expect anything. I just take the leftovers. I'm the garbage picker of life. Doris, I'm sick and tired of it. I will be going to Chicago, and I, damn well, will be having a great time."

"Nancy, what has got into you? I've never seen you like this. Something is terribly wrong. I think we should call Bob to come back home. You act as though you don't love your husband. The bible says that you should obey...."

Nancy cut her off in mid sentence. "Screw your convenient interpretation of the Bible."

Doris gasped and looked at Nancy in wide-eyed wonder. "You need to pull yourself together. Bob would be very upset if he heard you talk like this." She took her cup to the sink in an attempt to get her bearings and stall for a minute.

"Doris, I think our conversation is over. I've made up my mind. I will be going to Chicago on the weekend. You can ask Bob to take you to Rockford on Saturday."

Doris grabbed her purse and ran squarely into Melissa Perkins as she forcefully swung open the screen door. She huffed at Melissa in an annoying way, deliberately saying nothing. Doris mumbled something on their way to her big white Cadillac that sat in the driveway.

Melissa pulled up a chair and she sat across the table from Nancy. "By the way you look, it was a knock down, drag out."

Nancy's heart was regaining a more normal beat. Melissa had a way of calming. "You always seem to know exactly when to show up. I think that I've totally lost my mind. I did something today that I've never dreamed of doing. Trust me, I'll have hell to pay, later. I'll give you the short version. I told Bob and his demonic mother that I I will be going to Chicago with you to visit

Eden McNeal. I've never defied Bob. I hate to think what he is going to do."

"Honey, I'm so proud of you. This has been a long time in coming. If it gets too bad, you know that I've got a sofa for you to sleep on. You can call me anytime, day or night."

"Melissa, I doubt if it'll come to that. But I really appreciate your support."

"Let's not talk about anything negative. We both need to get away. It'll be so much fun. I've got a few bucks stashed so don't let that hold you back. It'll be first class all the way. Mike offered his car, but mine is okay. I just had new tires put on last month. Let's leave on Friday, say about three."

"God, you have no clue how much I dread tonight. Bob is going to make my life a living hell. I am sure that Doris will give him her version over the phone and it won' be pretty. I've never been anyplace without him. I want to eat out and shop, but most of all, I want to see how Eden lives. The curiosity is eating me alive. Promise me that your won't let me back out."

Nancy turned around and gently took her teapot off the shelf. She thought it was ironic that it was a gift from Doris. The decorative teapot looked like a little English cottage.

"Melissa, look what I've saved in this thing."

Melissa reached into the opening and pulled out a thick roll of bills. On closer observation, she realized that they were mostly hundred dollar bills. "How in the devil did you manage that? There's got to be thousands here. We both know that Bob isn't exactly a generous kind of guy."

"It started out as a game. I thought of it as my little secret. It took years, a little bit here and a few dollars there. As much as I hated to admit it, even to myself, I called it my escape fund. I used coupons, bought generic and poured the cheap stuff in the expensive containers and Bob never caught on. It was exciting to know that at least I had control over some tiny part of my drab nonexistent life."

Melissa clutched the impressive wad of bills with a puzzled look displayed on her face. "I don't half understand what you're saying. I'm so confused. You're going to have to pin point communicate with me. Are you saying that you're fed up and plan on leaving Bob?"

"Sometimes when he is especially abusive, I lie in bed planning my escape. Of course, in the morning it's business as usual. You know that I don't have the backbone to do anything. But I do have my stash of money just in case."

"Nancy, something happened today. I've never seen you stand up to Doris or Bob the way you did this morning. What's going on with you?"

"It was Eden. We haven't seen her in years. She's so self assured and beautiful. I was angry for letting myself become Bob's slave. It all came to a head this morning.

Melissa, I feel like I'm consumed with misery, living my life in a cocoon. It's a good thing that Bob went to work when he did. I'm ready to blow."

"Honey, take some advice from an old veteran. Stick to your guns but keep your mouth shut. If you feel that you need to talk, talk to me. We both know that you're not going to change Bob so don't waste your breath. I have to tell you what my fortune said in one of those fortune cookies. It said that a fool reveals all of his opinions. I'm trying to tell you not to say anything else to Bob about this trip to Chicago. And Friday, before he gets home from work, adios Roberto."

TWO

Melissa

"So, out with it. Did Jeff Phelps hit on you last night?" Mindy, Melissa's co-worker, slid a cup of coffee under Melissa's nose. She was speaking to woman who was too tall, vibrant hair that was too red, a face with too much make-up and a personality too gregarious. She thought that in spite of all that, Melissa Perkins looked damned sexy.

"Shut up. If he did, do you think I'd tell you?" Melissa laughed, and then cringed as she took a big gulp of the bitter black coffee. "This stuff sure the hell doesn't improve with age. I'll tell you one thing though, that red dress you lent me sure worked. Those bald married men were drooling all over themselves."

"Come on, Melissa, I know that you came to work early because you knew I wanted all the dirty little details, so out with it. I'll bet you were the youngest looking woman at your twenty-fifth."

Mike Casey, the second of Melissa's three exs', was having his breakfast at the counter just as he always did three mornings a week. "Mindy, she might not have been the youngest looking, but she was sure the sexiest. Red hair, red dress, va va va voom."

"I don't want to bore you with the details. I haven't seen Eden McNeal since high school, talk about looking good, she's still a size two and wrinkleless. I guess that says something about never being married and not having kids. That's got to be the key."

"What's she doing now?"

"She sits on the board of directors of one of those big companies in downtown Chicago and she lives in Oak Park. The best part of the reunion was she invited Nancy and me to spend next Friday night and all day Saturday with her. I can't believe that we're actually going to do it. Mindy, will you work my shifts? You know, you owe me big."

"You know I will, but that's not the problem. How do you think poor Nancy will pry herself away from that bastard husband of hers? There's no way that Bob will let her go. You're going to be going to Chicago all by yourself."

Mike looked up from his greasy eggs and sausage. "Somebody should break that ass hole's ribs."

Melissa threw her head back and laughed, her red curls dancing in the motion. "That is your answer for everything. Ever think that might be why we're not still married?"

"Before you go in, you better take a crash course in big words. Eden McNeal lives in another world." Mike reached over and fondly patted Melissa on the behind. "I'll give a night course if you're interested."

"How's this for a big word, sick-o-o-o. Tell me when you see Bob's car over at the agency. I need to pay Nancy a visit. She'll need some moral support." Melissa was now behind the counter helping out. She poured the stale coffee into the sink.

"She'll need more than a little moral support. She needs her head examined for marrying that jerk in the first place." Mindy paused in her arduous task of filling peppershakers. "I wonder if he ever abuses her."

Mike opened his tattered billfold and took out a ten. He generously dropped it on the counter. "I doubt if that coward would risk beating her, but he sure lets her have it with his mouth. Melissa, how are you going to get in there? Your car is a piece of shit."

"Nancy's got that almost new Explorer. That is if Bob will let her use it."

"Don't let that hold you back. You and I can trade cars this next weekend. I don't mind if you take mine into Chicago. It's hard finding your way around in there. I hope she gave you good directions to her house."

Melissa extracted a neatly folded paper from her purse, which was stowed discretely under the counter. "Mike, these are the directions to Eden's house. She went into great detail and insisted that it's an easy trip. Thank God, she gave us both her home and cell number. Will you take a look at the directions and give me some pointers?"

Mike deposited his massive body back down on the metal stool. "Babe, you've gone to Woodfield shopping. That's where you get off. Look here, it's almost a straight shot. These directions are great. She lives in Oak Park, how ritzy is that?"

"Besides, Eden said that if we get nervous, we could pull into Woodfield, call her, she would come and get us. Seeing her was like old times. I wish we would have all stayed closer."

Mindy chimed in. "I'd bet you my last dollar that you'll be going in by yourself. Nancy won't have the balls to stand up to Bob. Besides, you are long overdue for a vacation. Just tell Donna that you're going to take a whole week off. You know that she won't give you a hassle and we've got the coverage. I told you that I'd work this weekend and any other hours you might need me for next week."

At eight o'clock sharp on Friday morning, Melissa's phone rang. "Hey, are you packed?" Nancy's voice sounded up-beat.

"I can't believe that you are really going to do it. I guess I'll be sure when that Explorer is heading down the highway."

Nancy chose not to respond to her last comment. "I know we planned to leave at three, but do you think we can leave earlier? I'm packed and ready. I have my suitcases hidden under the bed, and, as luck would have it, Bob left early for the office. I'm so excited. I got the Explorer gassed up already this morning."

"What's Bob going to do when he finds out that you drove?"

"Do we really care?"

"Pick me up at noon. I told Donna that I'd waitress until noon. Then we can be off. The only thing is that Eden won't be home until six. Hey, don't worry about that, we can shop in those expensive little shops in Oak Park until she gets home, maybe even have a café latte at Starbucks. You'd better not change your mind between now and noon."

"Oh, my God, we're really going to do it."

At exactly noon, not one minute before or one minute after, Nancy pulled into the parking stall in front of Donna's Diner. When Melissa loaded her single suitcase into the back, she couldn't help but notice the size of the four pieces of luggage that Nancy had already deposited. They were all huge. Melissa laughed when she closed the door, and they slowly pulled out of the drive. "Sweetie, there's no room for my suitcase. What's up, are you moving out?"

"Maybe."

All the way down highway I-90 the two women talked and laughed. Nancy commented. "I haven't laughed like this since high school."

"Make a promise to yourself that this is the way that

it's always going to be. Nancy, you didn't bring that big wad of money, did you?"

"I sure did."

"Was that smart?"

"Yup, it was definitely smart."

"Did you leave Bob a note with Eden's phone number?"

"No. I left nothing. In fact, I even took the cell phone." Nancy paid a toll and then pulled off the highway. She took the phone out of her purse and dialed, obviously she got the home answering machine. "Hi Bob, I'm on my way to Chicago. There's some hamburger thawing, and I made a salad that's in the fridge. Be back soon."

Melissa looked a Nancy awestruck. "Be back soon? Why is it I feel like we're on a Thelma and Louise kind of trip?"

Nancy laughed. "Maybe it's because we are." Then she became serious. "Somehow I feel as though I'm at the crossroads of my life. I really don't have to account to anybody."

"We're going to have several hours with nothing to do. Let's find Eden's house and then go shopping. What do you say?"

"I say that I've got an agenda. I've already decided what we're going to do when we get to Oak Park and I'm not going to tell you 'til we get there."

Nancy, for the first time in years, felt as though she was in charge.

An hour and a half later, Eden's detailed directions in hand, the two women pulled into the driveway of a large, expensive Oak Park English Tudor house. "Oh my God, this can't be it." Melissa spoke in a highly excitable voice.

"Right street and right number. Yes, I'd say this is it. She must have a gardener. There isn't a weed that would dare grow in that yard. Well, now we know where it is, so I can take you on my secret quest."

They drove down the main Oak Park street, Nancy looked to the right and left. "Ah, there it is, right where she said it was." Nancy, expertly parked the SUV close to the curb. "Well, you'd better get out, Melissa. We can't be late for our appointments. By the way, I made one for you, too. Actually, Eden did. I phoned her on Wednesday."

"You are full of surprises. I don't know if I can afford to get my hair done in this fancy place."

Nancy pulled a credit card out of her purse and laughed so hard that a lone tear ran down her face. "Compliments of Bob."

The salon was something out of a movie. Neither Nancy nor Melissa had ever had an experience like that one, black, gold, plush and expensive. The staff was dressed like they were going to a formal party. Melissa laughed out loud when the receptionist offered them champagne from hand cut crystal glasses. When the experience ended, they climbed back into the dark blue Explorer.

Melissa was the first to speak. "At least, I still look like the same person. Which is something I can't say for you."

"Well, what do you think?"

"I think that you've totally lost your mind. We definitely left the old Nancy in Rockton. Honey, you look like a million bucks. It had to cost a fortune but so worth it. Make-up, manicure, cut, but best of all you're a blonde. Let's go all the way and stop at one of these tata little shops and get you a new outfit."

"Let's. We have a glorious hour and a half to spend some more of Bob's hard earned money."

"I don't mean to throw cold water on your little adventure, but do you have any idea how much trouble you're going to be in?"

"Melissa, I never thought I would see the day when I'd be turning to you to be my conscience." Nancy laughed as she playfully rubbed her friends strong shoulder.

When at long last they pulled the Explorer into Eden's driveway, Nancy was sporting an expensive new dress. Melissa refrained from spending any more money, but it didn't matter. She was satisfied with what she was wearing.

"It looks like Eden made it home. Her Mercedes is in the drive."

"Oh, my God, it's not just a Mercedes, it's a silver Mercedes convertible. It just keeps getting better and better. I can't wait to nose around inside that house."

THREE

Eden

Justin Phillips poked his head around the heavy oak door. "Can we go over the agenda for this afternoon's conference?"

Eden McNeal attempted to eat a sandwich and talk on the phone at the same time. With her hand, she motioned Justin into her considerable, professionally decorated office. The view of Lake Michigan was spectacular. Eden was uncomfortably aware that Justin was looking at her shapely, long legs as she sat on the side of her desk. She took the opportunity to tug her skirt down as she placed the phone back on its cradle.

Justin knew, as he looked at her, if she was a little younger and many inches taller, she could easily be a model. Her olive skin and black hair gave her an unmistakably exotic demeanor. Eden had strikingly good looks with a face unmarked by age. Anyone, who came in contact with Eden, knew that she was a woman to be reckoned with. Her size had nothing to do with the power that she wielded and everybody who came in contact with her, knew it as well. Neither man nor beast could ever succeed in taking advantage of her, as Eden McNeal was a powerhouse in a size two body.

"What?"

Justin was so deep in thought that he was caught off guard at her directness. "Sorry, where do you want the conference set up?" He hoped that his face didn't mirror any signs of redness.

"I don't care, use your own discretion. Just let me know so that I'm not running around here like a fool."

Eden's eyes were large, dark, and intense. Her shiny, almost black hair was cut stylishly short in what would be referred to as informally perfect. Nobody had any idea of her nationality, being impossible to discern. In fact, she would appear amused when anybody tried to guess. Eden McNeal was described as mysterious. McNeal, a Scottish surname, would typically be their first guess, although she definitely didn't look like a Scott. She always smiled and reminded them that she changed her last name after college for professional reasons. As she would be free to admit, for an escape from the past.

Justin was about five years Eden's junior. He was tall and slender with a refreshing ruggedness about him. No matter how close he shaved, his dark beard was still visible. He wore his hair a little too long, which added to his mystique. Justin was said to be handsome by many women, but Eden never gave him a second look. It was over a year ago that he was hired as Eden McNeal's assistant and he considered it an honor.

"You shouldn't be eating those poisonous sandwiches from the deli."

"It's this poisonous sandwich from the deli or nothing. It's not only Monday, but it's developed into the day from hell. Usually, the insanity doesn't start until at least Tuesday."

Her words came quick and crisp, something she learned from years in the business arena. Time is a precious commodity that better not be wasted. Work was her life, so that brisk quality spread to her private life.

"Justin, you know that I've got a dinner meeting with Lyle Goldman and Cliff Burkhart. They're only going to be here one more night. This is my only chance. If I don't, I'll be stuck flying to LA to finish up. And we both know that is not an option."

"Okay, where do you want reservations and what time? Are you going home to change first? You don't have anything dressy enough here at the office. Remember, you changed here last week and wore that dress home."

"Seven-thirty at Collette's should be fine. Justin, I hate to do this to you again, but I don't have enough time to go home. Obviously, I can't wear this navy suit. I need shoes and a dress." Eden handed him her Nordstrom's charge card. "You know all my sizes. Listen carefully. This time, no straps anywhere, on either shoes or dress. I hate brown, crayon colors, pink, or red. Read my lips, nothing to accentuate my cleavage. Take note, there is nothing on the upper part of my body to work with."

Justin tried not to smile, with not much success. "Why the complicated instructions? I did brilliantly last time."

"Justin, I really did appreciate your effort and your enthusiasm. But this time, do you best not to make me look like a trollop. Work somewhere within the boundaries of Mother Theresa and Madonna, that's all I ask." She picked up her phone and began to dial. Eden hesitated for a moment. "Justin, if you want to join us, make the reservations for four."

He turned quickly, being careful not to let her see the edges of his lips turn up as he exited her office. He had no time to ask her about her weekend class reunion even though he was enormously curious. Justin let his thoughts run rampant. Maybe after dinner they would have a chance to talk about some personal things. Eden might even invite him back to her house for an after dinner drink. He was shocked back into reality when he bumped squarely into Linda Gerson, knocking her into a wall, papers flying in every direction. Linda was single, attractive, and visibly attracted to Justin.

"I was having a bad day until now." She brazenly flirted with him from under her long dark lashes. Linda noticeably left her hand on his arm a moment too long. "Why don't you pry yourself away from that witch of a boss long enough to take me to lunch?"

"The last time I looked Ms. McNeal was not witchy. Do any of you women like her?"

"What's to like? She's bold and aggressive, plus worst of all, size two, without trying."

"If Eden were a man, you wouldn't use aggressive and bold. You'd use the words, assertive and strong. I think you women are your own worst enemies."

Linda pushed her hair off her forehead. "Don't find yourself getting too attached to her, Justin. She's living with some old fart named Victor and they've got a big house in Oak Park. I hear he's got lots of money, in fact, he's loaded. It's a good thing he's rich because word has it that he's definitely not very attractive. I heard he is as ugly as shit."

"Linda, I've met Victor. I wouldn't believe everything you hear. Women find him extremely good-looking and he's somewhat younger than Eden. I don't have time to talk. I have to go. But it was nice running into you."

Linda turned to watch him quickly walk down the corridor. She shook her head and resigned herself to picking up the three envelopes that she dropped in the collision.

Even though the week flew by quickly, Friday turned into an exceptionally long day. Eden was determined that, no matter how hectic today became, she wouldn't abandon her goal to be home at or about five-thirty. She looked so forward to seeing her two old friends. Justin suggested that she take them to a downtown tapas restaurant. Eden agreed that Meson Espanola would be perfect, informal, and yet different. Yes, she was certain that neither of her friends had ever experienced Spanish cuisine. Tapas would be the perfect informal meal.

Victor stood nearly motionless as Eden pulled into the drive. He watched her from the long narrow living room window, slowly turning when she walked through the sunroom into the kitchen.

Eden immediately said, "Don't even start on me, I know I'm late and you're hungry."

Before Victor could respond, the doorbell chimed. Eden virtually ran to the door, leaving him alone with a bewildered look on his face. She flung the heavy oak door open and pulled Melissa and Nancy into the entry hall. They, all three, spoke at once. Victor stood, patiently watching the frantic scene.

"I would like to introduce you to Victor, the man in my life. Pretty pathetic, isn't it?" Nancy and Melissa laughed as they bent down to pat the fat gray striped cat's head. With a swish of his tail, the cat padded out of the room. "Nancy, what happened? I wouldn't have recognized you. My God, you're not only blonde, but you're wearing make-up."

"Eden, I went to your hairdresser, who was a magician. Look, I'm a new woman." Nancy turned in a circle displaying her new hairstyle.

Melissa added, "She certainly is, in so many more ways than you can even imagine."

"If you want to bring in your things, I'll show you to your rooms. If you hurry, we'll have time for a drink before we go to Meson Espanola."

Melissa commented. "I love Mexican food but it might be a little hot for Nancy."

Eden closed her eyes and shook her head. "Melissa, what am I going to do with you? We aren't going to be eating tacos tonight. Meson Espanola is a Spanish tapas restaurant. It has nothing to do with Mexican food. Spain and Mexico have an ocean separating them. Tapas are out of this world appetizers. Then, of course, the fruited

wine, sangria. I promise, it will be quite an experience."
At that moment, Eden knew why she didn't make
reservations at an upscale restaurant.

The staircase wound into the entry hall, but both
Nancy and Melissa couldn't resist the temptation to
sneak a peek into the living room. Her eyes were wide
as she discovered every unexpected surprise. "Eden,
this looks like something out of House Beautiful. The
colors are so rich and warm, it feels like you could be
wrapped in them. Bet you used a big time Chicago
decorator."

Nancy was rightly impressed that the strange colors
seemed to work, cinnamon, cocoa, gold and maroon.
The inside of the house was reminiscent of the outside,
English Tudor. There was a carved stone fireplace that
would be spectacular on a cold winter's night.

"No, I didn't use a decorator. I thought that I could
pull it off as long as I kept it simple. Remember, I'm color
blind." Eden laughed and rolled her eyes to the ceiling.
"Sometimes it works to my advantage. When you're color
blind, all colors match."

"Nancy is into the antiques. I generally hate them,
but this looks good. You sure have a lot of room for you
and Victor. Why such a big house?" Melissa talked as
she walked into the study, which was through the
double French doors at the end of the long living room.

"I do quite a bit of entertaining for the company, but
the real reason is investment. Houses here in this area,
well, you know, it's an investment. Enough, go get your

suitcases. If you keep yapping, we won't have time for a margarita."

Eden escorted her two friends up the winding oak staircase to the spacious four bedroom upper floor. The continuity of the Tudor style flowed into the bedrooms and bathrooms. "Nancy, get your butt in here. You got to see this." Melissa was standing in the middle of Eden's master bath. "This is bigger than my whole apartment." The floors were stone and the cabinets were done in the dark English wood. The tall narrow window at the end of the bath was gracefully curved. Even the upper floor had coved moldings, which seemed to make the ceilings and walls flow into each other. They were most amazed with the extravagance of detail everywhere. "I feel like I'm in a castle in England."

When Nancy and Melissa were settled in their separate bedrooms, they finally came downstairs. Eden had already made a pitcher of margaritas and was pouring them into salt-rimmed glasses. Nancy thanked her and took a substantial sip. "So this is a margarita. I've never had one, but I'm sure I can grow to love them."

Both Eden and Melissa laughed. "We're going to have to keep our eyes on her tonight. Make-up, blonde hair, and margaritas, tell me that's not a lethal combination."

Nancy sat with her head back and her legs stretched out on the rich mahogany leather ottoman. She closed her eyes, trying to imagine that Rockton was a place in one of her recurring bad dreams, not a place to where she would ever return.

FOUR

The top was down on Eden's convertible, so Nancy sat in the front seat. She didn't want the wind to ruin her new hairdo. The night air was delightfully warm and Eden took a long route along Michigan Avenue and Lakeshore Drive to their final destination, Meson Espanola. The beauty of the buildings bedazzled Melissa and Nancy.

"Looking up at these buildings from a convertible gives you a whole new perspective. The tops of these buildings are so ornate. Each one of them on its own is a work of art. I have a new appreciation for the beauty of Chicago. Eden, do you ever park this car and go down by the water? Lake Michigan is so beautiful."

"Sure, I like to ride my bike here on the weekends. On Saturday mornings I come here to run. The breeze from the lake is wonderful."

Nancy felt mellow from the large margaritas. She was glad they didn't go directly to the restaurant. She needed some time for the drink to wear off, feeling as though time was passing in slow motion. "I think somebody else has inhabited my body." Nancy spoke softly, not intending for anybody to hear her.

Melissa heard her. "I think you're right, but I prefer the new Nancy. She's a lot more fun."

Eden was occupied as she looked for a parking space, constantly dodging traffic. She was barely aware of the conversation, deciding to let the valet park the car to save them a considerable walk. The building was a surprise. The front of the building was nice but not impressive. The impressive part was the crowd of buzzing, happy people. It was an enormously popular restaurant, but fortunately the owner knew Eden. He spoke to her, laughing and conversing in Spanish as he escorted them to the best table in the place. With his compliments, Jaime sent over a large pitcher of sangria and a plate of Spanish bread with olive oil for dipping. The waiter also spoke to Eden in Spanish, she ordered something, and he left.

Eden took a long sip of her sangria. "Okay, what are you two in the mood for? We'll order about five things and then share. Tapas are like appetizers, but far better. I know you will love the food, so it really doesn't really matter what you order everything they serve is wonderful."

"Eden, why don't you order for us? Surprise us.Is that okay with you, Nancy?"

"Sure, I could sustain myself on the fruit in this fantastic wine." She giggled.

"Oh, my God, Nancy is getting blitzed. She's giggling

like a ten-year-old. Just order, we need to get some food in her."

Nancy reached for the pitcher of sangria to help herself to another glass. Eden swiftly grabbed it and slid it away. All three women laughed.

Like magic, right on cue, the waiter appeared. Eden spoke to him in flawless, fluent Spanish.

As soon as he was out of earshot, Melissa spoke. "Well, what are we having? I can't even read the menu."

"Your memory is shorter than Nancy's. Remember, you told me to surprise you." Eden shook her head, laughed and took another sip of her sangria.

"I haven't had so much fun in a long time." Melissa slipped another piece of olive oil soaked bread into her mouth. It seemed to melt on her tongue. "What is this magical stuff?"

Eden replied, "Olive oil."

Nancy's face became visibly sad and her lips started to quiver. "I have never had so much fun."

Eden took note of the quivering lips and decided to change the mood before Nancy would spill some liquor-induced tears. "Well, you two, our fun is not even close to being finished. We have tonight and all day tomorrow. It's our job to make the best of it." Conversation slowed when the massive amounts of sumptuous food began to arrive.

Nancy thought how personable it was, passing plates of food, the sharing among friends. "What's this that I'm eating?"

"Octopus." Eden said nonchalantly, without even looking up. "How do you like the salmon with the capers and dill sauce?"

Nancy's mouth hung open. "Wait a minute, back up. You just said octopus, I don't eat octopus."

Eden laughed and laid down her fork. "You also don't drink margaritas or sangria. Now you have added octopus to your new long list of new experiences." She promptly put her hand over her glass when Melissa attempted to serve another glass of wine. "I'd better not, driving downtown is pretty hairy even without all this sangria. I'm going to stay sober, at least until we get back to my house. What's wrong with Nancy, two drinks and she's out of it?"

Melissa served herself another helping of the paella. "Bob never let Nancy drink, so she's not used to alcohol."

Nancy said offhandedly. "Bob says that I am stupid enough without booze. I wish he could see me now. I'll show him 'stupid'. Let's call him." Nancy clumsily reached into her purse and retrieved the cell phone and dramatically began to dial.

Eden gently slid it out of her hand. "Let's not dirty our evening with Bob's ranting. But it might not be a bad idea to check your messages."

Nancy obliged and listened to her messages. She had three, all from Bob. "The man is mad." She handed the phone to Melissa and redialed so she could hear what Bob had to say.

Melissa looked at Eden. "He's threatening to call the police to report the Explorer stolen. What a bastard."

Eden frowned, as she waited to speak. "Willy Krupke couldn't still be Rockton's police chief? He'd have to be older than God."

Nancy shook her head in affirmation. "Should I call him and tell him that I am safe and sound in Chicago? Bob said that he was going to report me missing."

Melissa took the phone and got Chief Krupke on the other end. "Chief Krupke, this is Melissa Perkins. Nancy Benson and I went to visit Eden McNeal in Chicago. If Nancy's husband Bob tries to file a missing person report or stolen vehicle report, it's bogus. She's sitting right her beside me all safe and sound."

"Actually, Bob did call me. Put Nancy on the phone, I need her social and driver's license number."

Nancy gave him all the necessary numbers, but she refused to relay Eden's phone number or address. Eden was puzzled by her attitude. "Why don't you cooperate, Nancy?"

"Eden, Willy wouldn't hesitate to give Bob your address and phone number. He's one of the good old boys. I don't know what my plans are yet. Even if I did, I have no intention of tipping my hand. For once in my life, I'm 100% in control, and it feels so good that I plan on making a habit of this. I can't believe that Bob would file a police report and have me arrested. He's taken this control thing to an all-new level. I don't think I've ever been so mad at him. Look at you, Eden, why haven't you ever married?"

"It's a proven fact that single women have fewer mental health issues than their married counterparts." Eden took a delicate bite of her dilled salmon and capers, closing her eyes to savor the flavor.

Nancy was amused. "Cop out. Now answer the question, Eden."

Eden was silent for a moment. "I didn't want to. Besides, why would I need a man? You two were privy to a lot of misery that I, obviously, avoided."

"Okay, Nancy, it's your turn. Why did you marry Bob?"

Nancy took a deep breath as though she was about to dive into deep water. "Fair enough. Bob is about four years older than I am. I was flattered that he was showing so much attention. I am going to divulge a dark secret. I was pregnant and pretty much railroaded into that marriage. Not that I minded. I thought Bob would be a great husband and father. He always worked hard and was a good provider. But, two months after we married, I had a miscarriage. He hit me once when I called him a reincarnated Nazi. He was so stingy and possessive. It happened so gradually, the way he got stronger and I got weaker. Guess it was safer and easier giving in. You know me, I was never much of a fighter."

"This place is noisy, let's go back to my house. I'll make another pitcher of margaritas, and we can stay up all night if we want to. It'll be like an overnight, just like the kind we had when we were kids. At least we won't have annoying parents telling us to be quiet and go to sleep. Is there anything else you would prefer, wine, beer or martinis? We could stop at the supermarket and get some fruit. I know how to make sangria if you'll cut the fruit."

"Yes, for margaritas. What's your vote, Melissa?"

"Those margaritas that you made earlier were kick ass. Let's rock on. Do we need to stop for more tequila?"

"I keep my liquor cabinet bursting. No, we don't need to stop."

As Eden drove into the garage, she looked at the moon, it was nearly full. The night had a strange foreboding feel, almost mystical. They entered the house through the sunroom door. The lights came on brightly, as they were on sensors. Eden's sunroom was all glass and octagonal shaped. Those lights also came on as they stepped into it. Even the ceiling was glass, which gave the moon even more prominence.

Melissa turned around twice, surveying every square inch of the space. "Let's get into our pajamas and drink our margaritas in here. What kind of a room is this?"

Eden laid her keys on the desk. "It's an octagonal room. Actually it's a conservatory, but I like calling it my octagonal room. It has a kind of exotic feel to it. I can think better here than any other place."

Nancy slowly counted the glass walls. "It's so big and it's long, but you're right, it does have eight sides. It unquestionably qualifies as an octagonal room."

A half hour later, the three friends were drinking margaritas and eating tortilla chips with salsa in the enormous glass room. The space was immersed with tropical plants, which included tall banana trees, palms and fragrant gardenias, which gave off an intoxicating scent.

Nancy couldn't stop talking as she tried to take in every detail. "Everyplace I look is dessert to my eyes. Eden, I am so glad you didn't give in to wicker furniture."

Eden couldn't help but laugh. "I'm not a fluffy kind of girl. Wicker doesn't work for me. I was all about comfort, and I never thought that sitting on pokey sticks particularly comfortable."

Melissa rubbed her slippered foot across the brick floor. "So you think that brick all about comfort?"

"Don't give me a hassle about that brick floor. I put a soft lush area rug in here, so as not to offend your delicate feet. Besides, if I carpeted it, you wouldn't be able to enjoy the whirlpool. Just sit, you'll find the furniture pretty comfy. This isn't the greatest place in the winter. It gets pretty drafty but it's sure nice the other three seasons. Some days I play hooky from work and sit out here with my computer, Victor, and the phone."

"Don't be surprised if Bob shows up, maybe even tonight. I'm so glad you let me put my Explorer in your garage. He has a way of getting any info he needs from anybody. I'm kind of scared to go home."

Both Melissa and Eden got serious, but said nothing. They just contemplated the words for a minute. Finally, Eden slowly spoke. "Nancy, there is a reason, only you know, that you put up with this for so long. I'm not here to throw cold water on this evening, but maybe in some minuscule way, Melissa and I could help. You know, even though it might look like it, I'm not a totally self-obsessed woman. I'm very fortunate, but I do try to give back. I volunteer to counsel abused women. I've seen it all. There is nothing new or shocking that I haven't heard."

Melissa's expression was clearly pained. "She has to pretend that she doesn't even know me. If we see each other, it has to be in secret. Bob hates me so much that he won't let Nancy talk to me."

"Won't let? I have heard those two words so often. It's like the mantra of abused women." Eden refilled the three salt rimmed margarita glasses. "What if he does show up, Nancy? You know Melissa and I will do anything we can to help, but we can only do so much."

"These wonderful little drinks are giving me false courage. If he came her right now, at this very minute, I would threaten him with the police if he didn't get his butt out of here."

"And tomorrow?"

Nancy's eyes were lifeless and cast downward onto the large cocktail table in front of her. "I've come to a fork in the road. I'm so sick of lying about what I'm doing and being evasive." Nancy began to weep. Her shoulders shook as she continued. "All my life I was abused by men. It began to feel natural."

Melissa moved closer to Nancy on the deep sofa to put her arm around her. Nancy instinctively flinched. "Bob has been more than just verbal. He's been hitting you, hasn't he?"

"Yes, yes, now you know. For a long time, he had me believing that I asked for it."

"And you don't believe that anymore?" Melissa thought that Eden was being too brutal and direct. "What did you mean when you said that all your life you were abused by men? I don't understand, I remember your father, he adored you. He seemed to be the quietest and most sensitive man ever born. Was I missing something?"

"My father was wonderful. I don't want to talk about it. These margaritas are making my tongue slippery."

"No, Nancy, you're not getting off that easy. If this is a fork in the road, let's leave all the litter at the fork and continue fresh."

FIVE

The back of Eden's neck prickled in anticipation of Nancy's next words.

"Stop pounding me about my past, or I'm going to throw up on your expensive oriental rug." Nancy's eyes grew too bright and her voice too shrill. She picked up her glass with an unsteady hand.

It was unusual for Eden to pound so hard on personal issues. "Don't try to shift the focus. For God's sake, Nancy, just relax. You're here among friends, just let it go. You can't let the past rule the future."

The phone on the end table began to ring. Eden answered it and then got a puzzled look on her face. "Where did you get my number? It's not published." She put her hand over the receiver. "It's Bob. Do you want to talk to him?"

Nancy's eyes grew large with fear, as she shook her head no. "Nancy doesn't want to speak with you. She says that she'll phone you at her convenience." Eden paused while she listened to Bob Benson. "I realize that if you have my phone number, you also have my address. I'm not stupid. Shut up, Bob, it's not necessary to recite it. No, you aren't going to force Nancy to talk to you. I believe that your days of forcing her to do anything are long gone."

Nancy gently took the phone from Eden's hand. She reluctantly put the receiver to her ear. "Bob, stop yelling. No, I'm not coming home right now. It's almost eleven o'clock. Please go to bed. I promise that we'll talk tomorrow." Nancy listened patiently for an additional two or three minutes, without saying anything. "No, I refuse to come home tonight. In fact, you can go straight to hell as far as I'm concerned. I doubt if I'll ever come home. Threatening to come here to pick me up will bring you an unpleasant surprise. Eden will call the police and I won't stop her. I think this conversation has ended." Nancy hung up the phone, her eyes reflecting the terror she felt.

Melissa and Eden watched the performance in awe. Melissa applauded, crossing the room to give her friend a supportive hug. "Honey, I'm so proud of you. This was such a long time in coming."

"Melissa, what makes you think that what just happened could possibly have been positive. He's a violent man, and unfortunately he's probably on his way here as we speak."

Eden walked over to her alarm system control box to double check it. She opened the writing desk drawer and took out a revolver. "Nancy, we are in control. And, I don't mean just for tonight. Bob will not hurt you again, not unless you allow it."

"I've pushed the envelope tonight. I've really pissed him off. I'm afraid that there's no turning back now. I'm worried that he'll do something crazy and put us all in danger. Nobody says no to Bob."

"Nancy, I put a state of the art security system into

this house. It would take somebody a lot more savvy than Bob Benson to get through it. Are we going to let him ruin our evening? You know that's his goal."

Melissa poured herself another drink and returned to the sofa. "Can we at least go into the living room? I feel like a sitting duck in this big glass room."

Eden's eyes were intense. "No, absolutely not. We will never let any man intimidate us again. We are three strong women, not sniveling weak little pukes." She picked up a tortilla chip and dipped it into the salsa defiantly. Victor yowled in agreement, or maybe it was simply a loud yawn. "Nancy, it will take a man a hell of a lot bigger and stronger than Bob to intimidate me. Besides, we haven't finished our talk." Eden noticed that Nancy was looking rather dazed, although, it didn't prevent her from pouring herself another margarita. "Nancy, before Bob called, you were about to tell us about the other abuse you endured before you were married. You insisted that it wasn't your father."

"Don't you ever forget anything? There is nothing that gets past you. How could there ever be three women so different?"

"Are we really that different? None of us have kids. None of us ever had a great relationship with a man. None of us has ever been totally fulfilled." Eden laid her head back on the soft slip covered chair before she continued. "It's pretty clear that we have more things in common than different. The only factor that makes me different from you and Melissa is that you two have spent your adult years trying to please men and might I add, with no success? I've never thought men were worth it. Let's make a promise to each other that we stay close and not split up again."

Nancy carelessly raised her half full glass, the contents nearly escaping. "I'll drink to that. Let's all use this night as a confessional. We'll all tell each other the reason why we are the way we are."

Eden laughed. "Okay, then let's start with you. You never did tell us who, other than Bob, abused you. Every time it's brought up you seem to get side tracked."

Deathly silence took over the room. Nancy began to sob quietly and then her sobs became uncontrolled. "I can't talk about it, I have never talked about this with anybody.

The wind caused a branch to scrape, like nails on a chalkboard, across the glass in that octagonal room. All three women jumped. Eden reacted quickly, heading for the gun in the writing desk drawer. "A little paranoid, aren't we?" Eden laughed. "Okay, Nancy, out with it. There will be no more interruptions. We're all going to confess things about ourselves tonight that we have kept deep in the confines of our minds. Nancy, were you raped in high school?"

Nancy's shoulders shook with even more uncontrollable sobbing. Then she silenced. She took a deep breath before she spoke. "No, I was not raped in high school."

Melissa put her arm around her best friend. "Thank God. You had us scared."

Nancy continued. "I was sexually molested in grade school."

You could have heard a pin drop in that glassed octagonal room. It was as though the glass of the room was symbolic of seeing into each other's souls. Eden got out of her chair and knelt in front of Nancy, still silent. She put her hands on Nancy's knees. Nancy appeared to be in a trance.

Melissa was the first to break the silence. "Mr. Anderson?"

With the pad of her thumb, Nancy wiped away one of the tears that was streaming down her face. "How could you know that?" Nancy's face appeared almost childlike.

"Me, too." Melissa closed her eyes, in an attempt to shield herself from the pain.

Eden's jaw was set and her teeth clenched. "That fucking pervert got all of us."

They were so deep in the misery of their thoughts that the phone rang three times before reality hit. Eden hissed as she answered the phone. "Hello. Oh, shit, it's you again. Why don't you give it up, Bob? Just try it, I invite you. You, or no other man will ever control Nancy again."

Eden slammed down the receiver. The three women still sat in silence. They seemed not to care what just transpired on the phone. Bob's phone call was minuscule compared to what they had just shared. What was of premier importance a half hour ago was not even worth acknowledging now. They sat in absolute silence for an interminably long period of time, all encased in their own version of hell. Sickening flashes of horrific memory and guilt threatened to engulf them.

The only sound that cut through that intense silence was Victor's purring on the back of the sofa. "We could have dealt with this so much better if only we could have confided in each other." Nancy knew the discussion was predestined.

Melissa said soberly. "We were in third grade, and he threatened to kill my parents if I told anybody. Besides, I thought that I was the only kid in the world that this happened to. I don't know how you two dealt with it, but I blanked a lot of it out. I thought I was bad. I made up for it later on by trying to please men, lots of men."

Eden stood and returned to her chair. "And I decided to be so strong that no man could penetrate my life or body again. I studied and pushed myself beyond all limits, as I attempted to never need a man for anything. I am totally self-sufficient. No man will ever need to support me, not as long as I have a breath left in my body. My question is, 'why doesn't this anger and rage ever go away?'"

Nancy began. "That's where Bob came in. I married him for protection. He was strong and I was submissive. I would have given up my life just to please him."

Melissa patted Nancy's hand. "You did. I'd like to know how many other little girls did that bastard molested. He had a perfect opportunity as a third grade teacher for all those years."

"You two live in Rockton. What ever happened to him? Jerry Anderson must be retired by now. I guess that he'd have to be in his mid to late sixties."

"I'll bet that Nancy knows where he is. Bob held the insurance policy on the drug store after he bought it. He got bored with the drug store after he retired and moved up into Wisconsin somewhere. He and his wife, Phyllis, bought some cabins to rent out near some lake, I heard. A good place for the son of a bitch, out in the woods and away from people. Nancy, where exactly did he go?"

"I can't remember. I'm good at blocking things out. After he cancelled the policy on the drug store, Bob still insured the cabins for about a year. Then he transferred the policy to a local Wisconsin agent. I have always kept the books for Bob's agency so I had to deal with all of that. I felt like I was in my own private hell."

Eden was intense again. "Can you find it on a map?"

"Who cares?"

"Can you find it on a map?"

"I don't know, maybe."

Eden unfolded a map of Wisconsin. She stood over Nancy. "I don't know, Eden. This has been such an emotional night. I don't think I can handle much more of this. What's the obsession about finding Jerry Anderson? Why do we care where he has his cabins?"

"You two have been staring at that damned map long enough. Eden, it's after two in the morning. Nancy is practically cross-eyed. I think we should go to bed and you can start this inquest again in the morning."

"Eden, you are so closed mouthed. What's that all

about? Why do you even care where Jerry Anderson is?"

"We're gong to confront him, that's why."

Nancy's voice was frantic. "No, no, we're not. I can't ever face that monster again. I can still feel his hands and smell his stinking breath. No, we can't...."

"Nancy, there are three of us. I think it's time we confronted our demons." Melissa looked tired and battered. Her voice cracked as she spoke.

"Don't I have any say in this, am I invisible? I confronted Bob. One demon at a time is plenty for me. Besides, we are leaving tomorrow, I mean today."

"I'll tell you what the plan is." Eden folded the map and laid it neatly on the desk. "We're going to bed. If either of you need a sleeping pill, I've got plenty and I'll be glad to share. I'm setting my alarm for eight. Nancy, you will be clearheaded in the morning. I'm telling you, we are going to find that bastard. No matter what it takes."

SIX

Melissa heard a gentle knocking on her bedroom door. "Melissa, the coffee is on and I've started making breakfast." Eden walked into the room and sat on the edge of her bed. Melissa could smell the strong aromatic coffee that permeated the house. "I wanted to talk to you before I woke Nancy. Is she going to be okay with going to Wisconsin?"

"This isn't exactly a vacation. I don't know, Eden. She really went through hell last night. We've got to keep in mind that her whole life has been turned upside down. I think that she finally let go of that joke of a marriage. There is no way that she can ever go back now. Being away for such a long time, you don't know Bob like I do. You have no idea how brave Nancy was to do what she did."

"What about you?"

"I completely agree with you. I've always felt like I needed to confront that fucking pervert, but I just haven't had enough time to prepare for it. Until last night, I didn't think that he hurt any other little girl. I guess that was just one more thing that I needed to block out of my mind. Don't you think it is too soon? Maybe next month or possibly in a couple of weeks. That will give us some time to plan for...."

"Stop. Don't go there. We are going to do this. If it is ever going to be done, it has to be now."

Melissa defiantly stood with her legs spread in a defiant stance, her hands on her hips. "Eden, this is Saturday. What do you think we are going to do, just climb into the Explorer and head to Wisconsin? We don't even know what lake or what town, for that matter. For somebody who's so smart, you're talking crazy."

"We need to be strong and united for Nancy. Right now, because of the circumstances, you and I are stronger than Nancy. You are her only close friend. Melissa, it is up to you to bring her around to our way of thinking."

"Eden, I'm not sure what our way of thinking is. I don't even know what you're planning to do to Mr. Jerry Anderson."

"What ever we do, it will be as a joint decision, I promise. I have no plans. Melissa, all I know is that I have to make him accountable. I have to see him and talk with him. It is the only way I'm ever going to become healthy."

Neither woman heard Nancy walk into the bedroom. "My head is the size of a beach ball. Eden, I hope that coffee that I'm smelling is strong."

"Come on, let's get some breakfast in us."

Melissa and Eden refrained from talking about Jerry Anderson while they ate the Denver omelet that Eden expertly prepared. They filled their plates and ate their breakfast in the octagonal glass room. It was a little after eight and the sun already poured in. It was as though nothing ever happened just the night before.

"I can't believe that in spite of all the hell I went through yesterday, I slept like a baby. I swear Eden, you should patent your margaritas and sell them as medicine."

Melissa groaned and pushed the stray red curls off her face. "I don't think I ever want to hear the word margarita again."

"Come on, you wimps, we have things to do and places to go."

Nancy shook her head. "Eden, tell me you aren't still on that finding Mr. Anderson kick."

Eden laughed and began to clear the table. "Nancy, you have to help locate him. Try to remember. If you honestly can't figure it out, you have to think of a way that we can find him. We're leaving it up to you to solve this mystery."

"Okay, Eden, suppose we do figure out where he is. Then what? Let's talk about it. After all, I have nowhere to go and nothing to do. Remember, I no longer have a marriage or a home in Rockton."

"Nancy, we are a team. And a formidable team, I might add. Melissa and I aren't going to leave you all alone in the wilderness. We are both here to help you through this. You can stay with me here in Oak Park. Most importantly, we're not going to let Bob terrorize you anymore."

"Eden, I don't even have a job, let alone any training

to do anything. Bob never let me continue my education or work for anybody but him. I kept the books at the agency, but that's all that I've ever done. Who in his right mind would ever hire me?"

"I have a lot of pull and know a lot of people. Just trust me. You're smart and talented, it will be easy for you to find a job. Besides, you have me to help you. In fact, we are looking for somebody right now and I know you'd qualify for that job. A year from now, you're going to look back on this morning and wonder what you could ever have been apprehensive about. A year from now, you are going to have all your confidence and self respect back."

Eden laid out the map again and playfully pushed Nancy's face onto it. "Okay, okay, I get it. My mind is clear this morning, so maybe we'll have some luck. Oh, my God, I thought Minnesota was the land of the lakes. Wisconsin is just peppered with them."

"Nancy, concentrate on the towns not the lakes. Do you remember, at least, if it was half way up or all the way to Lake Superior?"

"I don't know. I told you that I blocked a lot out of my memory. Wait a minute, Eden, I think that I have a way of looking it up on the computer. Go get me your laptop and log me onto the Internet. I'm pretty sure that I can figure out how to find it."

Ten minutes later they had an address and phone number. "Nancy you are the queen of all computer geeks." Melissa was dancing around the glass room, still in her fuchsia pink cotton pajamas.

"You better change you clothes, Melissa. The old lady

who lives next door is always leering out of her window. If she sees you dancing around in your pajamas, she'll go into color shock." Eden tried to be serious but couldn't erase the grin from her face.

"Eden, how many times has Bob called?"

Nancy was filling the dishwasher. Her eyes were downcast. "Who knows? I shut off the ringer. I'll check my messages if you want me to."

"No, let's not."

Eden took her cell phone from her purse. "I'm going to call Jerry Anderson at Wilderness Lodge to reserve a large cabin for us for one week. Do you think that will be long enough? I want to be in agreement before I do it. I plan to use a phony name, and my cell phone will not show my name just in case he has caller ID. This like we discussed, is a team effort. Everything that we do will be agreed upon among the three of us. Are you ready for me to make the call?"

Nancy put up her hand in a stop position. "Wait. Let's talk more about it. Jerry Anderson knows Melissa and me. Remember, when we arrive, there will be no more surprises. You know, Eden, a week is a long time. Are you going to be able to swing it?"

"Don't worry about me. Melissa needs to call the diner to see if she can be covered. Maybe it's best to get that handled before I make the phone call to Wilderness Lodge."

Melissa said, "Don't give it another thought, I have

so much vacation time coming that I'll never be able to take it all. Nancy, it's you that we're concerned about. This week will be the deciding factor in your marriage."

"That's a done deal. I want to divorce Bob. This visit just pushed me over the edge. I think that I made that decision a long time ago but didn't know how to finish it. Thank God for you two. You gave me the courage to do something that should have been handled years ago. I just needed a little moral support."

"Nancy, you don't look or sound like the same person who left Rockton."

Eden held the phone in her hand. "Here we go." She dialed and waited. "Hello, is this Wilderness Lodge? Great, this is Beth Nelson from Chicago. Do you have any openings for a cabin for three women? We'll need it for one week. As soon as possible. How did I get your name? From the Chamber of Commerce. I have two friends who will be joining me so we'll need three beds. We are looking for something starting tonight." Eden made a pained face and waited for the response. "Wonderful. We will be there later, probably after dark. We are going to leave as soon as we get ready." Eden pulled out a pad and paper. "Okay shoot. I'm ready, give me the most detailed directions possible. Are you the owner? Great, see you later." The duration of the phone call was about five minutes.

"Oh, my God, were you talking to him?"

"No, it was his wife, Phyllis. Finding it is going to be

interesting. It's in the middle of nowhere, and I want it to be dark by the time we get there. We have to make about ten turns into the woods on single lane roads. We'd better load up quick and get going."

"Eden, load up what?" Nancy was looking at her with a confused look.

"Oh, crap." Eden started to laugh. "You didn't bring anything but city clothes."

"Melissa commented, "And we sure the hell aren't going to be able to borrow anything from you unless you wear your clothes three sizes too large."

"I'm not going to invest a lot of money in stuff for the woods or jeans. It's going to be cold up there so we'll need some sweat shirts and jackets. Let's head for some cheap place on our way out of town. It will probably take all day to get there, so we can't waste much time shopping. Why did you make reservations for a week? Do you really think that we'll be gone that long?"

"I don't know. We might need more time, or possibly less time than a week."

"What about Victor? You can't leave that fat cat for a week without food. I'm sure he's not much of a woodsman." Melissa was already starting up the stairs.

"I have a housekeeper who comes three times a week. She always feeds Victor. I'll leave her a note. Nancy, are you going to give Bob a heads up?"

"No. He doesn't need to know where I went. We have enough complications, without him on our butts.

Actually, I have no intention of ever returning to that house except to retrieve a few of my belongings. I knew what I was going to do before I left Rockton. I opened my own checking account and took half of the money out of our savings. I'm pretty well off. I knew the minute he figured out what I was up to, he would freeze all the accounts. That's why I want him to think that I'm coming back. Although, he will figure it out soon enough. Otherwise he will cancel the charge card. I might act naïve, but when it comes to money, I'm pretty savvy."

"Good girl. Grab underwear, toothbrushes, and whatever else you can use and throw them into your suitcases. I guess I'll be able to do some proper packing. I have all kinds of gear that I use when I go white water rafting.

Melissa gave Eden a mock curtsy. "As usual, Her Majesty will look sensational, and we'll look like a couple of slugs."

"Time's a wastin', let's get what we have into the Explorer. I think we should bring a cooler and stop at the supermarket for wine, pop, beer, ice, and sandwich fixings. We can eat on the road. It'll take hours to get there so we won't have time for food stops."

When the explorer was packed and they were ready to pull out of the drive, Eden needed to run back into the house to pack the coffee pot. But the coffee pot wasn't the only thing that she retrieved. She took the revolver from the desk drawer in the octagonal room and put it into her oversized designer leather purse.

SEVEN

Eden volunteered to drive, all agreeing that it was a better idea for her to drive through the city traffic. All three talked at once and were in the process of making plans when Melissa screamed. "Oh, my God, that's Bob. He saw us, I know he saw us."

"Are you sure?'

"Yea, he's trying to turn around. We're so lucky that there's a lot of traffic."

"We're lucky that I'm driving. I can lose him, no problem." Eden quickly turned onto an Oak Park side street and pushed heavily on the gas pedal.

"You better slow down, or we're going to have a cop after us."

"Melissa, be quiet and let me deal with this. I know what I'm doing. Nancy, quick, get Bob on his cell. Be extremely careful not to let him know that we are headed for Wisconsin. Tell him that we are going to a concert at Navy Pier and then out for lunch. Make sure that you let him know that we're running late. That's why we can't stop to chat with him. And for God's sake, be sweet. One look inside and he'll know that we're up to something. He better not have got a good look at your hair. Hopefully that will get rid of that ass hole. Be nice,

we don't want him canceling that precious credit card."
Eden made a sharp turn, and they parked comfortably
behind a big stone church.

"Yes, Bob, we did see you. No, of course I'm not trying
to avoid you. It's late and we are afraid we're going to
miss the concert at Navy Pier. We've been looking
forward to it. I think it will be late, Eden made plans for
the whole day. No don't be silly, of course you can't
come with us. It's a girl's only day. Of course, I didn't
bring much money. Eden treated us to a wonderful meal
last night and wouldn't take a dime from me. I'm thinking
that I want to spend another night, depending how late
we get back to Eden's house. Don't act like that. We're
just having a good catch up. I'm sorry that your mother's
sick. I don't know Bob, if she's so sick, why are you
chasing me around Chicago? Go on back to Rockton, I'll
be back soon. I'm not sure, either late tonight or sometime
tomorrow. Bye." Nancy put the phone back into her
purse. "How did I do?"

"Great. Now we have to sit here and wait until the
coast is clear. We sure don't want to bump into him
again. We've still got three stops to make, the
supermarket, discount clothing store, and wig shop."

"Wig shop? Are you nuts?"

"Look, Melissa, we need to cover our bases. Jerry
Anderson will never recognize me after all these years.
But he lived in the same town with you and Nancy. We
need to protect our identity as long as possible and, if it
takes something as simple as a wig, so be it. Nancy is

perfect with that short haircut and blond hair, but he could see you coming a mile away with your long red curly hair. Don't ever underestimate that hair of yours."

"So the frigging wig is for me. I hate to bring this up, but I'm not exactly rolling in bucks."

Nancy laughed. "Again, compliments of Bob. We have to use that credit card as much as possible as long as we can. I plan on buying your new wilderness wardrobe with it, too. As soon as we head for Wisconsin, I'd better put it away. I don't want him to trace our trip with the charges."

They pulled into the back parking lot of the wig store. "We are only going to be a minute and please, Melissa, let me choose it. This is not to call attention to you. It's going to be straight, brown, and plain."

Ten minutes later, back in the SUV, Nancy commented. "Melissa, with sunglasses, your own mother wouldn't recognize you."

Eden looked at her watch and frowned. "We didn't count on that delay because of Bob. We have to make up the time somehow. I'm going to drop you two off to buy clothes and pick you up in a half hour. While you're doing that, I'm going to get our bug repellent and groceries. I also need to drive through the bank. Once we get to Wisconsin, it will be cash all the way, no checks or credit cards. Within forty-five minutes, we should be heading north. And Nancy, I hope you had the good sense to turn off your cell phone."

"God, Eden, you're beginning to sound like a drill sergeant, lighten up."

When Eden picked up Melissa and Nancy, they were standing inside the entrance of the building, just in case Bob was still skulking around. Eden laughed when they finally emerged. They had so many bags that they virtually were forced to drag two of them. There were far too many to carry. "We spent a fortune. Nancy insisted on going first class all the way."

Nancy laughed so hard that a tear rolled down her cheek. "I can't help it. Bob's a big spender."

"You've got everything now? You bought shoes, underwear, socks, jackets...."

Melissa interrupted. "Eden, we split up and bought everything in sight. It took two carts. No, we didn't forget anything. Nancy even bought the dorkiest looking hat on the planet."

"Oops, I just about forgot." Eden took out her phone and dialed. "One more call. Justin, I'm glad I caught you. You need to cancel some meetings for this next week. I won't be there. No, everything is fine. I want to spend some time with my two friends from Rockton. If a guy named Bob Benson calls, tell him that I am on a business trip and you don't know when I'm returning. Yes, Justin, I remember the Wednesday meeting with.... No, I don't. Listen to me, take care of it. Just cancel everything and I'll be back in a week. For once, I am going to put my own personal needs in front of those of the company. I can't talk, I'm heading into traffic. Take care and I'll see you in a week or so."

"Who is Justin?'

"He is my guardian angel. Actually he is my assistant and he's wonderful."

"How wonderful? What's he like in bed?"

Eden couldn't help but smile. "Not that wonderful. I leave him at work."

"What movie star does he look like?"

Eden just shook her head, not answering.

Melissa said in an exaggeratedly whiny voice. "I have to go to the toilet."

"God, you're impossible. Can you at least wait until we get out of the city? I need to gas up, and we can stop in a half hour. Is that okay?"

"I guess."

Not much was said for the next half hour. Nancy even dozed off for about twenty minutes. The landscape changed drastically once the blue Explorer crossed the Wisconsin border.

"I bought some sandwich stuff, fruit, and pop. I put it all into the cooler. I even remembered plastic silverware and paper plates. Let's drive for a while further and stop for a picnic. I'm getting kind of tired of driving."

"I'll drive next." Melissa was chewing some spearmint gum much too loudly.

"Not if we want the tires to hit the road. Melissa drives like a mad woman." Nancy checked her watch and looked again at the map. "We're making great time. I don't know why we're in such a hurry, you've got the cabin reserved. I'm sure they're not beating off prospective guests with a stick."

"No, it's not that. I'm not too excited about arriving in the middle of the night. Driving down those deserted roads, not knowing where we're going wouldn't be too smart. Besides, as far as I'm concerned, I just want to get it over with."

"Get what over with? I'm not clear on anything, Eden."

"We'll firm things up while we're eating our lunch." Eden swerved to avoid a squirrel. "I'm a city kind of girl. Where did all these beasts come from?"

Another hour passed and Melissa spoke. "Two big issues, I'm hungry and I have to go to the toilet again."

"What's wrong with you? Is your bladder the size of a pea? Let's start looking for a place to picnic. I saw some signs for a state park. It should be coming up soon. What's this? Here is." Eden parked as closely as she could to a picnic table. They scrambled out of the vehicle, all doing a separate task. The food was simple and to the point, and the day was brilliant. The sun was shining through the branches of the big oak tree that shaded their table.

Nancy commented. "For the world to see, we look like three good friends having an uncomplicated picnic on a beautiful summer day. How deceiving."

Melissa said, "We are."

"Not quite. We are three close friends, in macabre fashion, on our way to raise havoc with our molester." Eden's face mirrored that intense look.

"What exactly do you have in mind, Eden? I'm not sure what raise havoc means?" Melissa reached for another grape, popping it into her mouth.

"You know, Melissa, I am not really sure either. I just know that Mr. Jerry Anderson's free ride is over. He's about ready to reap his come upance."

"Eden, you have made much more complicated plans than either Melissa or I can even imagine. The wig, your reluctance to discuss it. There is a lot more going on in your head than you're letting on. You said that we are a team. Well, it's time you passed the ball. Melissa and I are two thirds of this team. Keep in mind that we were on the receiving end of that pervert's hands."

"Do you two feel ready to discuss what happened all those years ago or do you still want to keep it all tucked safely inside?"

Melissa looked away. "Eden, I don't know if I can."

"Then I'll start. You two protected yourselves by blocking things out. I blocked nothing out. My memory is crystal clear and vivid. Every detail is engraved deeply in my mind. He told me that he was my teacher and every good little girl did what her teacher told her. He said that he had only my best interest at heart. He made me go over to his house right after school, and if I didn't he said that he would hurt my mother and father. He showed me a long sharp hunting knife that he kept in the back of his kitchen drawer. He said he would slit their throats if I wasn't a good little girl and kept my mouth shut. Sound familiar to either one of you?"

Nancy put her hand over her mouth and ran into the trees. Eden and Melissa could hear her as she vomited. Eden held Melissa back when she started to get up from behind the picnic table in an effort to comfort her friend.

"Leave her alone. Melissa, we all need to come to terms with it in our own way. Please, you must give Nancy this last small piece of dignity."

EIGHT

Melissa did most of the cleaning up and loading the remnants of their picnic. Nancy looked white and frail as she sat in the Explorer. She patiently waited to leave. Eden took a pen and traced their route on the map. Very sparse words were exchanged as the resumed their exodus north. Melissa drove and Nancy occupied the other front seat. Eden, instinctively, handed her a bottle of cold water.

"Nancy, I know these have been the most gut wrenching couple days of your life. I don't want to appear brutal with my directness, but if you really feel you can't deal with what we are about to undertake, please say so. You've been through so much and I don't want to push you into some kind of a nervous collapse. I would never forgive myself if I were the reason that you went over the edge. Just say the word and we'll turn this vehicle around and go right back to Oak Park. You can wait for us at my house with no questions asked. But just tell me."

Tears welled in Nancy's eyes. "I can't believe you said that. All this plotting and planning we have done together, and you'll deposit me back in Oak Park? All this because I tossed my cookies in the woods? I never would have had the nerve to confront Jerry Anderson on my own, but now I'll be with the two people I trust most in the world marching beside me. There are a lot of tasks in life that aren't easy but still have to be done. I am sitting here quietly because I'm weak, that's all. I'm not angry, I'm not pouting, I'm where I need to be, beside my two best friends. Eden, it was you who said that we were a formidable team. I probably won't be able to contribute as much as you two, but I want to be there doing all I can."

"Okay, I get the picture. But, I hope at some point you'll share your experience about Jerry Anderson. I think you need to come to terms with it. You'll find it cleansing, but I won't push you right now. In fact, I won't even bring it up. By the way, you look like shit."

If you two don't mind, I think I'll take one of my migraine pills. I'm going to need to sleep for about an hour or the pill won't work. Just give me my hour and I'll be a new woman."

Melissa pulled the Explorer to the side of the road, and Eden took Nancy's place in the front seat. Within a few minutes, Nancy's soft snores could be heard in the back of the Explorer.

"Eden, you look at this adventure as therapeutic. I see it as scary. Nancy's asleep. Tell me what you plan to do once we get to Wilderness Lodge. You are the most intelligent person I have ever met, and you're such a pro with words. What I have seen so far is you side stepping every time you are asked. I'm going to ask you again and I'm going to keep asking you until you give me a straight answer. Eden, what is the plan?" Melissa spoke in an exaggeratedly slow manner, as though she were addressing some one with a decreased attention span.

"You know, Melissa, I have no idea. Like you, I'm just flying by the seat of my pants. I would like to recite an articulate and complicated strategy, but I'm in the dark too. I swear to you, what do I have to do to make you believe that I don't have a secret agenda? I'm not even sure if confronting him is the best idea. My practical voice tells me that attorneys, judges, and juries might be the way to go. You're right about Nancy, she has so much on her plate. It amazes me that she is as strong as she is right now. I have so much rage that it's hard for me to be sensitive to anybody. Melissa, you have no idea how much I've obsessed over the years with this quest of Jerry Anderson."

"Okay, I'll stop nagging about that subject. At least for now. Eden, this is going to be such a long drive, and I'm pretty sure that you're right that it'll be dark when we get there. I am so glad it will be late. I sure don't want to start anything tonight. Promise me, it's early when we get there, we'll waste time eating dinner in town or whatever it takes. I want to go right to the cabin and get a good night's sleep. None of use will be able to sleep very well, but I can't deal with anything else today. And, I'm sure that goes double for Nancy."

"I agree, today is not the day for confrontation. We need to do some serious thinking."

"I'm getting tired of driving, and we should gas up. I don't want to wake Nancy by stopping but…."

"Would you rather run out of gas out here in the boonies? Are you crazy, the red gas light is on."

"Where are we anyway? Get the map out and see if we're coming on any real towns. After all, Eden, you're supposed to be the navigator."

"The next little town should be coming up soon, Houghland. Good thing you drove, we covered a lot of miles. There it is, turn off at the next road."

They didn't notice that Nancy was now sitting up in the back seat. "This place looks like a Norman Rockwell picture. That little diner looks like it's open. After we get gassed up, I want a piece of Aunt Bea's cherry pie."

Eden smiled. "Are you sure you want to stop?"

Melissa discreetly reached over and pinched Eden's wrist. "Sure, honey, I'm ready for a break. A piece of pie and a cup of coffee sounds great."

The diner was straight out of the forties. One of the waitresses even wore a ruffled apron. "How long did I sleep? Or am I still having some weird dream?"

"The question is, how do you feel? You've got big dark circles under you eyes. I hope that magical triangular pill you took handled that migraine."

"Melissa, you worry too much. I'm much better, although I'm starved. Remember, I left my lunch in the woods."

All three women followed Nancy's suggestion and ordered Swiss steak, mashed potatoes, canned string beans and coffee. They ate in silence. Then a smile crossed Melissa's face. "Did Nancy tell you about her stash of money?"

Nancy slowly began the story. "It started out kind of innocently. I put it in a teapot that my nasty mother-in-law gave me. There was never a week that went by that I didn't stash some money that I frugally saved. When I was young and naïve, I told myself that I was going to surprise Bob with an exotic trip. I stupidly thought that an expensive trip would put some romance in that man's soul. I would lie awake at night planning exotic vacations. Sometimes it would be Bermuda and sometimes I'd envision a trip through Europe on the Orient Express. I would go to the library and get travel books. All the while, the money was growing. I thought how impressed Bob would be with this unexpected money that I saved. As the years went by, my fantasy was not with him. It was by myself. Then as more time passed, Bob kept getting meaner and meaner. That's when I began to call it my escape fund. God, Eden, I've saved thousands of dollars. Last week when Doris wanted a cup of tea, I nearly had a stroke. Actually that was the turning point. It was the day that I decided that I wanted out for good. Melissa, I didn't tell you, but those are not all hundreds. Some of those bills are thousands."

"Holy shit." The three of them had a good laugh. "Too bad that old Bob will never know."

"It's kind of a delicious little secret, don't you think?"

Eden looked serious. "I have an attorney friend who used to practice law in Rockford. When we get back, I'll call him. We'll hire the sharpest lawyer in Illinois. Like I said, we're a formidable team."

"Thanks for everything, Eden. We better get on the road if we're going to get there before dark." Nancy stood and swiftly sat back down again. "Every muscle in my body is screaming in protest."

"Eden and I had a discussion while you were snoring in the back seat. We decided that we didn't want to arrive in the daylight. We thought it would be a good idea to arrive later so we could go right to our cabin. Why deal with Jerry Anderson tonight? We'll be so tired, we won't be able to see straight. We sure don't want to make any mistakes at the get go."

"Good idea. Judging from the map, if we get there too early, we can go to one of the towns that seem pretty close. We used to go up north when I was a kid. There was a bar on every corner. I wonder if they just serve beer, or who knows, margaritas."

"I don't think I've been the greatest influence on you. Well, if you two are ready, let's get out of here." Eden grabbed the bill and left a generous tip. When they got outside, she took the keys from Melissa. "I'll drive. You said you were tired."

"What about me, I have not driven one mile. I feel better now, and I think I should do my fair share."

"Just get better. Nancy, sit in front with me and be the map-reader. This is going to be the hardest leg of the trip."

Nancy laughed. "Are we going to have a chance to drink our margaritas in Bear Junction?"

"You made that up." Melissa was adamant.

"No, I swear, here it is and it looks like it's the next town over from Wilderness Lodge. Besides, how could I make anything like that up? Judging from the time we're making, we will be at Bear Junction about eight. Let's stop and meet the locals. Maybe we can pump them about Jerry Anderson. You never know what we might find out. I wish we were just going on a little trip, not falling into this large black abyss."

After about half and hour, Melissa tapped Nancy on the shoulder. "My mouth feels like cotton. See if Eden has any mints or gum."

Nancy distractedly reached into Eden's black leather bag. When she felt the cold metal of the revolver, a startled scream escaped from her mouth. "What the hell are you thinking, Eden. Melissa, Eden has a gun in her purse. Are you planning on killing the son of a bitch?"

It's for protection, that's all. Think about it, we don't know who Jerry Anderson has become. He's had a lot of years to get even crazier. I will make both of you one promise. That is, that he will never have another opportunity to hurt any one of us, ever again."

Melissa's voice became agitated. "Just when I thought things couldn't get more depressing, here comes the rain. I didn't want to say anything earlier, but it seemed like we were traveling just in front of it. Too bad

it caught up with us. Eden, I don't know how you can
see a thing. It's coming down in sheets."

Nancy in one of her quieter tones said, "It's an omen."

"I'm going to pull over. I can't see anything." The
Explorer sat motionless at the side of the road.

"Eden, this is ridiculous. Get in the back seat. Sitting
at the side of the road is not going to get us to Wilderness
Lodge. I'm driving." Nancy spoke forcefully as she
opened her door, not giving either of them a second to
protest. Both Melissa and Eden thought how good it
seemed to have Nancy take charge. "Driving slowly is
better than not moving at all. Let's put some heat in
here, it's so damned cold I can nearly see my breath.
This will be a chance to decide on our new fake names,
we obviously can't use the ones we were born with. My
name is Ann, Ann Morton. How about you Melissa?"

"Hmm, I think that I look like a Marcy. How about
Marcy Hopkins?"

Eden laughed. "I don't have a choice. I already told
Jerry's wife that my name was Beth Nelson, so I guess
that's a done deal."

Eight o'clock found the women parking at Carl's
Place, in the small backward town of Bear Junction. The
rain proved to be relentless, never giving them a
moment's peace. The time of night wouldn't normally
have produced darkness, but the hour and the
combination of the rain left the atmosphere of the
parking lot dismally ominous.

NINE

When they walked through the well kicked, scuffed door of Carl's, they were greeted by the pungent order of cigarette smoke and stale beer. Loud laughter assaulted their ears. It took a few seconds for their eyes to adjust to the dim light and gray fog of smoke.

"This place is an armpit…. I can hardly see in here, I feel like I'm going blind. If you've ever seen Star Wars, this is the bar scene. Where should we sit?" Nancy moved instinctively toward the long unadorned bar. "If we want to talk to the locals, let's sit with them on the bar stools."

"Thank God, we're not the only women in here. This damn wig feels like a big tight hat. Eden, er, I mean Beth, you definitely don't fit in this place. Why don't you let me do most of the talking? It's a stretch to think that you could ever warm-up to these people. I've had more practice." Melissa plopped herself down next to a man in a red plaid lumberjack shirt and his blonde pony tailed friend. "Does it always rain in Bear Junction?" Melissa didn't wait for an answer. She proceeded to order beer for Eden, Nancy, and herself and continued talking to the couple next to them. "Wouldn't you know it, just when we can all get away for a vacation, it rains on our parade."

Eden couldn't help but laugh when the man in the plaid shirt introduced himself as Bob. She whispered to Nancy. "There are no coincidences."

Bob obviously forgot to shave that morning, or maybe that month. "This here is my girlfriend Tammy. Now that you know who we are…."

Melissa promptly introduced herself. "I am Marcy and this is Ann and Beth. We've been driving all day long. I've never needed a beer so bad in my life."

"All day, where did you beautiful ladies come from?" Eden grinned at his feeble attempt to be charming. It was clear that Tammy was not amused.

Nancy joined the conversation and Eden obligingly remained silent. "We're from Chicago, but we like to travel north to get out of the city. One of the guys I work with said he heard that Wilderness Lodge is a good place, so we reserved a cabin for a week. Now look, it's raining."

"So you've never been to that hell hole? You just chose a pig in a poke?" When Bob laughed, he threw his head back, and Nancy couldn't help but notice that there was a tooth missing in front.

"Glad to see you're amused. What's so funny about booking a cabin at Wilderness Lodge?" Nancy aggressively jabbed Eden in the ribs, reminding her to keep her mouth shut.

Tammy leaned toward Nancy to be better heard. "Just be careful, there's a weirdo who bought that place. You ain't there yet, why not go to Bill Dixon's cabins. They're closer and a hell of a lot nicer. Plus, Bill's a decent kind of guy. He's not an ass hole like that Anderson."

Bob shook his head in agreement. "Yea, he is a jerk, but I don't think he'd hurt anybody."

"Sure, Bobby, he wouldn't mess with you, but after a few drinks, he gets pretty mean. I don't think they should go. There is something strange about that guy. Remember when he came in here?"

Eden couldn't wait. She ignored another one of Nancy's jabs in her ribs. "What happened when he came here?"

"He put a lot of booze away that night. He got up on his high horse and told some of the wrong people that they were uneducated low lives. It was the beer talkin' but Jimmy took it to heart. So, they took it outside."

Tammy laughed so hard that she could hardly speak. "Anderson didn't even get in one punch before Jimmy beat his ass into the ground. His wife had to drive him home. I sure would hate to be her."

"Some of the people who come here are stupid, but it's not a good idea to bring that up. Jerry Anderson ain't been back since. He does all his drinking at Wilderness Lodge and he does lots of it, I heard." Bob took the last sip of his glass of beer. "Tammy's right. Why don't you cancel and go to Bill's place? There's something bad wrong with that guy."

"What's his poor wife like?" Nancy tried to act

nonchalant as she sipped on her glass of bitter beer. "Are they from this part of Wisconsin?"

"He says he was a teacher somewhere in Illinois. He's a mean dude. I don't think he should be around kids. It ain't just the booze. I feel sorry for Phyllis, his wife. It's like she's a prisoner there. She does all the work. She seems pretty much okay, not like him. Can't imagine what it's like being stuck out there with him."

Tammy wrote something on a paper napkin. She handed it to Melissa. "Here take this, it's my cell phone number. Bobby and I will help you guys out if you need us, feel free to call anytime. I don't mean to scare you, but you're better safe than sorry. Don't go there. Bob and I are here most every night, maybe we'll see you tomorrow."

It happened so fast that nobody saw it coming. A large burly guy with a black hat with a long feather grabbed Eden's wrist and pulled her onto the small dance floor in front of the jukebox. The sight had Melissa and Nancy in flabbergasted awe. At first neither of them could utter a sound. Then Melissa started laughing so hard and loud. "Oh, my God, Ann, I think that I'm going to pee my pants."

Tears of laughter ran down Nancy's face. The man with the feathered hat wore boots, which didn't help to make him any more graceful. He was now trying out some fancy dance moves. Eden's face cast in stone. Her dark eyes were unreadable, their only message, a strong warning. Nancy whispered to Melissa. "Shall we save her?"

"No, this is way too much fun. I wish we had brought in our camera. This is the stuff that blackmail is made from."

The big bearded man deposited Eden back on her barstool only after she was completely humiliated. She inconspicuously leaned toward Nancy and whispered. "He's inbred with about one chromosome away from insanity. Although I'm sure you can pronounce this evening a triumph. But, I've had enough fun for one evening. Maybe we should move on to Wilderness Lodge."

"How about another dance before we leave?" Melissa took the last long sip of her beer, draining the glass.

"Shut up, let's get out of this slime pit."

"You gals ain't never going to find Anderson's place in the dark and with all this rain. It's tricky even in the day. Tammy and I can take you there and wait 'til you get settled in your cabin. We can't let you go there alone."

Soon the blue Explorer was following the shiny black pick up truck down the narrow gravel road that wound into the Wilderness Lodge property. Nancy commented. "I'm glad our new best friends are helping us out. I'm not too sure we would have even found it tonight."

Eden was driving. She spoke with a sarcastic bite to her voice. "I feel an immeasurable sense of reassurance."

Melissa couldn't resist. "I know you're disappointed that Bubba didn't offer to tuck you in."

Eden pretended an attempt to push her out the car door. "Here we are, look at this dump. It's totally under whelming. I hope Bobby and Tammy won't just turn their truck around and leave. Let's ask them if they will wait until we get into our cabin."

When Eden stepped out of the Explorer, she stepped into a puddle of ice-cold water, which evoked more than a few foul words. She walked over to the driver's side of the truck and motioned for Bob to roll down his window. "I have a huge favor. Will you two wait till we get into our cabin?"

"Sure, we were going to do that anyway, Beth. We'll wait right here in the truck 'til you tell us you're okay."

Eden grabbed her purse from the Explorer. "Let me do this myself. Please stay in here." Eden paused to wait for the nods of affirmation.

It was all on large room. The reception area, the restaurant, and the bar, all crudely built with wood everywhere. The wood floors, wood walls, wood beams gave the room a dark and foreboding mood. The large stone-fronted fireplace held a small fire, which looked as though it were burning itself out. Phyllis Anderson stood in anticipation behind the crudely built reception desk. She was a petite woman, dressed simply in a denim skirt and a faded peach sweater. Eden wondered if her sweater had been orange, originally. No, she decided, Phyllis Anderson would never have been permitted to wear the color orange. Her hollow face mirrored the hard life that she lived. She stood there, her eyes vacant and deeply sad. She obviously stood at attention behind the poorly built desk because she saw the two sets of headlights as they wove up the drive. It took awhile for Eden's eyes to adjust. Only then could she see a lone figure of a man who sat at the far end of the desolate bar. There was a tall drink in front of him. Eden struggled to hide her own unease; her breath came short and shallow. He snuffed out his cigar, curiously stood and walked toward her, closing the distance between them. He was a more bloated and pasty man than Eden remembered. She remembered perfectly now, his lifeless gray eyes, his foul breath, and most of all, his gigantic rough hands. Yes, his was a familiar face in the dim light of Wilderness Lodge.

He spoke. "So you and your friends came here from the big city, huh?"

Eden had a nearly uncontrollable urge to pull the revolver out of her purse and lay him dead on the rough wood floor. She curbed her fury. The silence was suffocating as she starred at her nemesis. As though an evil fog were penetrating to her very soul.

"We're survivors here, how do you think you Chicago babes are going to do?"

"Looks can be deceiving. You can trust me, Mr. Anderson, we too are survivors. And you can count on us proving that to you."

"Miss Nelson, you have to excuse my husband. He's

had a hard day and it's late for him. He seems a little harsh after a drink or two, but he's a good guy. We'll do everything we possibly can to make your vacation enjoyable."

Eden knew that Phyllis Anderson's life was filled with the ugly task of making excuses for that pathetic shell of a man.

"I have to admit I'm exhausted and that rain didn't help. A nice hot bath along with a good night's sleep will do wonders for my mood. My friend, Ann, has a splitting headache. That's why she didn't come in. If you would just give me the key, I'll give you your payment and we'll be out of your hair." Eden took enough cash from her billfold to pay for two nights, neatly laying it on the counter. "Is there a restaurant close by? I have a feeling that we will be ravenous in the morning."

"Phyllis isn't famous for her culinary skills, but she can manage sausage and eggs." Jerry looked at Eden with a look of fleeting familiarity. "You're paying in cash? Cash patrons usually have something to hide. I'd bet that you're hiding from someone or something?" He then looked away. But not before he gave her a smug knowing look. "Give me the key, I'll take you to your cabin." He took the key from his wife and then stumbled slightly as he moved toward the door.

Eden was adamant and intense with her reply. "No, that will not be necessary. As long as there are clean sheets and enough towels for three women, that is all we need. Just point me in the right direction. I don't need your help getting there. Contrary to what you think, I am surprisingly capable."

TEN

It stinks in here. If it wasn't pouring, we could air this dump out." Melissa laid her suitcase on the double bed that was the closest to the window. The other two beds were singles. The crude cabin had only one redeeming quality, it's generous size.

Nancy propped her luggage against the middle bed and headed to the bathroom. "I think that ugly smell is coming from in here. Could be a dead rat. This bathroom is in a huge time warp, right out of the forties. At least we have enough towels and it seems somewhat clean. But, I'm still not putting my bare feet on this floor."

"There's no point complaining about it. We knew it wouldn't be the Hilton, so let's just make the best of it. It's so damn cold that I can hardly feel my fingers. Doesn't this dive have any heat?"

Eden was intent on adjusting the rusty thermostat that regulated the electric heat for the cabin. When it finally kicked-in, the lights dimmed and the noisy vents gave off a dusty odor.

"I've got a feeling that nobody's rented this cabin for months or possibly years. Maybe this will take some of the mustiness out of here." She began to peel off her layers of clothing, preparing to put on her pajamas. "Will you pull those ugly drapes closed? That pervert is and more decrepit. He was obnoxious and well on his way to getting drunk. I'm sure he didn't recognize me from so many years ago. He behaved like an arrogant old fool, of course, Phyllis made excuses for him. All the ugly memories flooded back the moment that I laid eyes on him. Blocking out all those horrific details saved you and Nancy, but my recollections are as clear as highly polished crystal."

"Are we going to eat breakfast there tomorrow morning?" Melissa was in the process of brushing her teeth and changing into her pajamas.

"Sure, how better to get to reacquaint ourselves with our attacker?" Eden had already put on her robe and pajamas. She sat on her bed with a pillow behind her back. "I saw a picture of a young light haired woman behind the desk. Do either one of you know who that might be?"

Neither Melissa nor Nancy said anything for a moment. They were both deep in thought. Finally, Melissa broke the odd silence. "Yea, that must have been a picture of their daughter. She would be quite a bit younger than us. I think she's married and lives in Arizona or Texas."

"Do you know her name?"

"No. You don't suppose that he molested her, too?"

"How can you analyze the mind of a mad man? The more we know, the stronger we will be. Can you think of anything else?"

Melissa prepared the coffee pot for the morning's brew. A thoughtful look transformed her face when she looked up. "Yes, I can think of something. How are we going to kill him?"

All three women jumped with the loud crash of thunder and the lightning that sooon followed, which illuminated the room with an eerie glow.

Eden took charge of the conversation. "Kill him? Now we're getting down to the business at hand. Melissa, climb into bed and stop acting like you're at the diner. My culinary skills are seriously impaired, but even I can make coffee in the morning. Right now, we have some important issues to sort through." Eden obliged by propping herself with two pillows and she covered herself with the faded blankets. "Nancy, let's start with you. How would you like to take care of Jerry Anderson?"

"I thought about this for a good part of our trip up here and definitely a good part of my life, as well. We could lure him to our cab in, shoot him and then tell the police that he was looking through our window. We could say that we mistook him as a prowler."

Melissa deliberated over Nancy's plan for a couple of minutes. She finally spoke. "I'd like to lure him to our cabin, chop off his dick and shove it down his throat." She looked from face to face, hoping to see some shock.

Eden obliged with a smile, but not with a response. "I have some medication that belonged to my mother that's not detectable. I thought to bring it with me, as a possibility. It's in my purse. If it were taken with alcohol, it probably would result in heart failure. Judging from Jerry's pallor and his big gut, it wouldn't take a doctor to see that he has some health problems. Wouldn't it be a shame if the bastard had a heart attack and we were here to enjoy it?"

Melissa became serious, which caused them both to stare. "Jerry Anderson isn't worth any of us spending even a nanosecond in prison. We've all suffered enough. The color of justice is green. But judging from this dump, old Jerry is not worth blackmailing. I say that we get him drunk and push him off the end of the pier in the middle of the night.. Who would know? There would be no witness, who would know? Eden, you used to be a lifeguard. You could be waiting in the water to pull him under."

Eden sat in a pensive mode thinking about Melissa's plan. Her eyes narrowed slightly. "Before we make any decisions, I want to know what we're up against. I want to know who and where his daughter is. I want to know what kind of relationship he has with Phyllis. I would like to bring Phyllis over to our side, without telling her about any plans of violence. We have a whole week and if we need more time, so be it. After all, we've spent a lifetime with this secret."

"I just hope when the bastard sobers up in the morning, he won't recognize Nancy and me. I always wear a pound or two of make up. Let's be honest, I'm pretty well known by my curly red hair. That straight brown wig and no make up should do the trick. Remember, my name is Marcy."

"I hope he isn't even there in the morning. With all the booze he drinks, I'll be he sleeps in. I would like us to get to know Phyllis without any interference from him."

"Didn't the Andersons move out of Rockton at one point?"

"Yes, they were gone for years. Then they moved back before he retired. Remember, they bought that darling little stone house on Martin Street? That's when old Mr. Harris died and the Andersons bought the corner drug store." Nancy patiently waited for the thunder to subside before she continued. "He was so unpleasant and bitter that the people didn't go in there anymore. Jerry couldn't figure that out. He treated his customers like shit and after a year or so, his drug store folded. That's when they moved up here and nobody much ever talked about them. The whole Rockton community was glad to be rid of him."

"What about his daughter?"

"Eden, like we said before, we don't know much about her. In fact, I forgot all about her until you mentioned that picture that you saw in the lodge. Speaking of the lodge, I dread seeing it for the first time tomorrow. At least you got that part out of the way. I sure hope it doesn't rain all day tomorrow. I can't think of anything worse than being stuck in that dismal place all day."

Melissa had to get out of bed to turn off the lights. None of the three women slept soundly that night. Eden was the first to awaken, relieved that the sun was trying to shine through the dirty windowpanes of their cabin. She had no idea that birds could be so obnoxiously loud. She watched her two friends as they continued to sleep. Under Melissa's hard-boiled exterior she had an innocent quality in sleep. Her red curls were plastered against her face, like a sweet little girl.Bored, Eden quietly walked to the bathroom. She paused to switch on the coffee maker as she passed. The water in the shower didn't get as hot as she liked it, but never the less it felt good against her skin. She wished that she could scrub hard enough to wash away all the guilt and pain from her soul. There hadn't been a day in her life that Jerry Anderson didn't haunt her thoughts and invade her dreams. Now, she thought, at long last, she would be able to get some closure. As she was fastening the belt to her terry cloth robe, she could hear Nancy and Melissa moving around and talking. She thought how tragic it was that the burden of Jerry Anderson had to come with her renewed friendship with Melissa and Nancy. Eden sat down on the toilet seat lid as she dried her hair. She was aware of the power she had over people. Eden knew how adept she was with words, how convincing she could be, like a master salesperson. She knew that she had to be sensitive to the desires of Nancy and Melissa regarding such a gargantuan issue. Whatever they determined to do with Jerry Anderson needed to be decided between the three of them equally. It would be difficult not to be in charge.

The tension permeated the cabin as the women proceeded with the chore of dressing. "At least the smell of the coffee takes the edge off the stink of the mildew. Eden, that coffee you brought is wonderful. I hope we have enough to last for the week."

"If we don't, we will have an excuse to shop in town if you want to call Bear Junction a town. I'm just teasing. We have more than enough, I brought two full bags." Eden's hair was dry, and she was completely dressed. "Remember, all for one and one for all. Can you imagine, no TV? Chicago could be blown off the face of the earth and we would never know."

"Let's not lose sight of our goal here, Eden. It's a great advantage. With no TV we will have more time to plan our action. Promise me that you will do nothing without the approval of Melissa and me."

"You have my word. I realize I'm used to being in charge, but I'll consciously try to curb that. We're a team, and team members work together. If I start to become aggressive and pounding my point of view, stop me. Sometimes I don't even realize I'm doing it. We need to make this a joint effort. Am I the only one of us who knows how to shoot a revolver?"

"Hell, no. After my divorce from Russ, remember I decided that I wanted to become a cop. I got half way through training and quit when I got engaged to Mike. I not only can shoot, but I trained in martial arts and can protect myself. It was one of the best things that I've ever done. But, like most other things in my life, I didn't follow through. So, I guess I am bringing a lot to this party."

Nancy looked down at the right floor. "I have nothing to offer. Eden has the brains, and Melissa has the brawn and I have nothing to bring."

"Honey, you keep this on an even keel. You keep us centered. We all have a job to do, and yours is every bit as important."

ELEVEN

A fog, a dense all consuming fog was the creation of the previous night's rain. Melissa hesitated before she put her foot out of the cabin door. "I feel like I've just landed the lead in a horror movie."

Eden laughed. "You did."

"'The eerie lavender stillness of summer'. I read that someplace."

"God, Nancy, you are such a dork."

They set off on their expedition down the long weed infested gravel drive. The three women said nothing as they entered Wilderness Lodge, each silently experiencing their own brand of dread. Eden opened the door and was the first to step over the threshold. Then came Melissa and lastly Nancy.

Nancy nervously whispered. "What a gloomy place. Let's order a lot of food and eat it slowly."

"Hey, there's nobody in here. I don't hear any domestic sounds coming from the kitchen or cooking smells either. Let's sit at that big round table by the window and wait." Nancy began to wring her hands.

"Stop that, at least pretend not to be terrified. Heads up, here she comes." Melissa had a fake smile plastered on her face.

Phyllis Anderson wore jeans and a faded navy polo. For a woman of her years, she looked surprisingly firm. It was her face that gave away her age. A gentle, but definite sadness haunted her, the look of a woman tormented.

"Which one of you had the headache last night?"

Eden spoke quickly. "Ann." She motioned to Nancy.

"I'm not only fine this morning, but ravenously hungry. Please don't go to any trouble, whatever you have is just fine. We don't want to cause you any trouble." Nancy's hand trembled slightly when she pushed the hair off her forehead.

"How about bacon and eggs? I'll be right back with your juice." Phyllis Anderson didn't wait for a response, turned and walked toward the swinging door to the kitchen.

"Still no Jerry. It would be great if we could convince Phyllis to sit with us. After all, this is an informal lodge, not a restaurant. Besides, we're the only customers here." Melissa turned to look out the window. "In fact, we are probably the only guests they have. I don't see any boats, trucks, or cars."

Phyllis wasted no time bringing the food. Eden looked at it and commented. "It smells so good. Please, fix yourself a plate and sit with us. We have so many questions about what to do while we're here. We would love to have you join us."

Both Nancy and Melissa smiled and shook their heads in affirmation. She discreetly looked around and probably lurking out there under our windows trying to sneak a peek." Even the thought of it, made her shudder, putting the hair on the back of her neck in a standing position.

Melissa laughed, doing a comical little dance in the middle of the room. "Said by the woman who insisted that we stay in her glass room because no man was going to intimidate her."

"This is the most butt ugly room on the planet, but it does have a fireplace. I wonder if it works."

"Hunters come here in the winter and there's even some logs. Why wouldn't it work" Once again Eden started poking around with their heating options.

The walls of the cabin were covered in knotty pine, all but one wall. That wall had wallpaper that was at least sixty years old in a dirty beige and brown cowboy motif. The floor had threadbare rust colored carpet.

"These bedspreads look like they went through a war." Nancy picked up the corner of it and sniffed. "At least they have been laundered. If this was a vacation, it would qualify as the vacation from hell."

"Eden, you promised to share what happened in the lodge when we got safely here in the privacy of this cabin."

"Both Jerry and Phyllis Anderson were there. Of course, he was his ever arrogant self. You two have seen him more recently than I have. I would have recognized him anywhere. I despise that man with every fiber of my being. He looked pretty much the same but much older walked slowly to the kitchen. A couple of minutes later she came back with a plate of food.

"It is so nice of you to include me."

"Honey, I for one need to talk to somebody new. Ann and Beth are starting to get on my last nerve." Melissa laughed and took a bite of her eggs. "Especially Beth, it's going to take a small miracle to turn her into a camper. On our way here, she called a squirrel a wild sharp toothed beast."

"So, I never pretended to be a woodsy mossy kind of gal?"

Phyllis looked down at her food and smiled. "I hope Beth doesn't run into a bear while she is here."

"Bears? Please tell me there are no bears." The color drained from Eden's face. "I saw a documentary once about bear attacks. I'd like to keep all my appendages, thank you very much."

"Just don't go wandering off by yourselves in the woods. We are extremely careful of disposing of our garbage. They don't aggressively hunt humans, the bears just want our food. If I were you, I'd be more concerned about ticks. Did you bring good repellant? Every night, do a tick check on each other. The deer tick has almost reached an epidemic. Don't trust your repellant. It helps, but it is not totally effective. Make sure you check each other every day, maybe even twice."

Nancy smiled and looked at the sensitive woman. She thought what a close parallel that she and Phyllis

Anderson had. Eden sensed what Nancy was thinking by the expression on her face.

Eden decided to break the silence. "Ann needed a break. That is why we came here. She just got out of a horribly abusive marriage. Marcy and I are so proud of her. We know that it takes a lot of courage to finally make the break."

Nancy knew that Eden had method to her madness. And at that moment, knew exactly what it was. Phyllis looked at Nancy with deep compassion in her eyes. "It must have been difficult. We all get so settled in our lives. It is so hard to make changes even if they are for the best. You are still young. It will be so much easier for you."

"What do you mean easier for you? Are you speaking about yourself, Phyllis?"

Phyllis Anderson looked vacantly at Melissa. "I didn't mean...I'm sorry, I've said too much. Can I get you more juice or coffee?"

"We're fine. Just sit and keep us company. My husband was abusive, and I was lucky enough to have two good friends to help me. I wish I would have done something before, but better late than never."

"Yes, you are lucky to have two good friends to help you through it. So many women don't have that luxury."

"Like you?"

"Why would you even insinuate that I have a problem?"

"Phyllis, I am an abused woman, and it takes one to know one. The look in your eyes is the same look that I had such a short time ago. I lived every day of my life unsuccessfully trying to make the bastard happy. At the end of the day, I came to realize that nobody can make another person happy. Happiness is something that is manufactured from within." The fork shook violently in Phyllis' hand. She laid it down and put her face in her hands. "Jerry says that nobody wants to hear about my sad life."

"Jerry isn't here, is he? Sometimes talking about the experience is liberating."

Melissa sensed that Phyllis was about to clam up with Eden's directness. Once that happened, they would be lost. "I've been married three times. Honey, I could teach you all something about how impossible it is to make someone else happy. In all seriousness, through all this I have learned one thing. Being alone doesn't mean being lonely. I am glad to pass that on because it took me a long time to come to terms with that."

Eden pointed to the picture behind the reception desk. "Is that your daughter or a picture of you a few years ago?"

Phyllis smiled and her expression softened. "We haven't seen her in so many years. She's always too busy to spend time here with us. I talk to her a lot on the phone though. Texas seems like a million miles away."

"Any grand kids?"

"No, Paula isn't married. In fact, no close calls either. She had a lot of dependency problems with drugs, gambling and alcohol. Thank God she got some help. I tried to save her, but Jerry was hopeless. She says that she's okay now. After graduation from high school, she packed her bags and never came home again. You have no idea how much I miss her."

She took a deep breath and swallowed. Phyllis had tears stinging to come out, but she refused to become emotional in front of strangers.

"Who do you miss so much?" The women were so deep in conversation that they didn't notice Jerry Anderson approach the table. "I need a cup of coffee, and I've got a headache, so get me an aspirin while you're up."

Melissa and Nancy sat in a stupefied awe at his presence. A wave of panic washed over Nancy. The bile in her stomach was fighting to get free. Eden motioned for him to sit. Then she got up and walked to the coffee pot.

"Hey, we're not going to let our guests wait on us. Get up Phyllis, and get me my coffee." He annoyingly tapped his fingers on the table. "Damn it woman, I told you to get up."

"Let Beth do it, she's got more energy than all of us put together." It was obvious that Melissa was trying hard to disguise her uneasiness. She thought that her heart was going to pound right out of her chest. "We need Phyllis here to tell us how to spend our day. She is going to be our tour director."

He sat, studying the women through his wire-rimmed glasses. His not so full head of hair, now with a generous speckling of gray, needed a thorough shampooing. It fanned out sloppily over the top of his ears, begging for a trim. His only redeeming quality was the clothes, which were clean and pressed, no doubt due to Phyllis' diligence. Melissa noticed that even though it was only a couple of years since she last saw him, he had aged considerably. She was convinced that the alcohol had taken a large piece of him. Still a sizeable man, he was beginning to hunch, maybe a touch of arthritis had set in. His eyes were still piercing, and his jowls were even more pronounced than she remembered.

The moment he saw Melissa, his eyes narrowed. "You look familiar. Have you always lived in Chicago?"

"Um hum, always. Born and raised in the same house, five blocks from Wrigley Field."

"I have met a lot of people. I'm sure everybody looks like somebody else. I was a grade school teacher. Retired now and glad of it." He looked in the direction of Eden, zeroing in, he continued. "Beth Nelson, huh? I don't think so. I'd sure like to know what you have to hide. Fake address and fake phone number, paying in cash? I wasn't born yesterday."

Melissa squeezed Nancy's knee under the table in anticipation of how Eden was going to counter. They knew her style and her intense temperament, making both friends cautiously nervous.

Eden casually finished chewing her bite of cold toast and calmly looked at him with an unreadable look behind her eyes. "Right you are Sherlock, but you missed something. Fake name, too, all of us."

"Well, out with it, Who the hell are you? I demand to know."

"We don't owe you anything, including money. You are paid for today and for two more days in cash. If this is such a respectable place that you need to know our history, I guess we can move on and find a place that doesn't. We noticed on our way here that it isn't the only lodge in the area. Are you still feeling as though you are having a problem with our anonymity? If you do, it will take us five minutes to pack."

Phyllis Anderson's eyes were wide and she fidgeted with the kitchen towel she held in her hand. Finally, she opened her mouth to say something but prudently decided against it.

He gave no indication that he heard what Eden had said. "Being hunted by an irate wife?"

"No, by an abusive husband. We were just discussing it with Phyllis before you appeared."

"What did you do, take the poor guy for all he had and then run away? My guess would be that you could make any man's life a hell with your aggressive attitude." He laughed at his feeble attempt at sarcastic humor.

"Right again, Slick. There is no man alive who could ever take advantage of me, or even mildly intimidate me. So, if that's your goal, give it up. Bigger and stronger men have tried and failed. And just for the record, I wouldn't be stupid enough to get married."

"What's your real name?"

"It's Beth and that's all you need to know. I'll tell you one last time, get off of that hot topic, or we'll pack up and leave."

Nancy was relieved that he selected Eden to spar with and not her. She studied Eden as she spoke to Jerry Anderson, thinking what a barracuda she must be in her professional life. Eden kept her emotions well concealed; her eyes and lips thin as she bantered back and forth with him, never once faltering. Nancy wondered if Eden had the revolver in her purse.

"Some guy must have got you real good to make you as bitter as you are."

"Right on. For once you're right. Some guy got me real good to make me the way I am."

Nancy thought it was all over. She had faith that Eden could control herself, but she also knew that Jerry was playing with dynamite. "So, Phyllis, is there any antique shop around here? Beth has a whole house full of them. It would be kind of fun to go antique shopping. Besides, I don't think Beth would appreciate hanging out in the woods."

"There are two or three right around Bear Junction. I could draw you a map."

"Is there any reason why you couldn't go with us after while?"

"I don't..."

"Yes, there is a reason why she can't go with you. She has work to do here. This is a business, in case you haven't noticed."

Eden pushed her chair away from the table. "Entertaining other guests? Seems to me that we are the only people staying here. Put the dishes in the dishwasher, and we'll pick you up in an hour." She turned from the table in an attempt to seal the deal.

"Jerry, I do have to by groceries in town. I am sure Beth wouldn't mind bringing back groceries." She looked to him for his consent.

Eden turned as she left. "See you in about an hour."

TWELVE

Just in case Jerry was watching from the bay window, they held their tongues until they got safely inside their cabin. Then it was utter chaos, all speaking at once. They decided not to give him any hints as to why they were at Wilderness Lodge. He was given nothing to whet his suspicions.

Once inside, they all voiced their ideas and their opinions. Melissa held up both of her hands in the stop position, to make Nancy and Eden cease their chattering. "Okay, we have an hour to cook up a plan. What are we going to do with Phyllis? Unfortunately, she isn't as evil as we hoped. That would have made it a hell of a lot easier."

"Eden, I could tell by your face that you have something in mind. This would be a good time to fill us in. Just keep in mind that we're a team, although I am glad that you took over the conversation with that bastard. I don't think either one of us could have done it."

Eden dismissed her vote of confidence. "Phyllis Anderson, what should we do with her? What do you think, Nancy?"

"Eden, don't pretend that you are even mildly

interested in what I think. Melissa and I know that you have something in mind, what is it?"

"Okay, you want me to go first? Nancy, you and Phyllis had a special connection for an obvious reason. I think that this should be mostly your job."

"What job? What are you talking about? You know, Eden, pinpoint communication is your special forte. What is wrong with you, now? Speak woman."

Eden did her best thinking in silence, but couldn't help but smile. I feel that your job will be to pull Phyllis over to our side. That just seems like the logical solution."

"Sure, that should be easy. Two hours in the Explorer and she will shed a lifetime of abuse and drive off into the sunset with three virtual strangers. For somebody so smart, you sure can be naive."

"Before Jerry Anderson interrupted, you were developing a repoir with her. We are going to be here a week or so. Today is just going to be a good strong beginning. We want Phyllis on our side, but whatever plans we make, we definitely cannot include her. Talk to her about your relationship with Bob. If you commiserate with her, you'll be able to instill her trust."

"Are we going to tell her that her husband is a freak?"

"Melissa, you have such a colorful way with words. You're right, we will probably end up telling her that her husband is a freak, but not today. It's far too soon. We're going to have to develop a trust first, and that's going to be Nancy's job. I have an idea. I hope that I can pull it off. If we can figure out a way to get Nancy and Phyllis alone, you are going to have to get her talking about her miserable marriage, Nancy. And you thought you didn't have anything to bring to the party. Honey, you are the one who is going to be the door-opener."

"I wouldn't be shocked senseless if Jerry wouldn't let her leave with us. Then what?"

"Let's not beg for trouble. If she can't come with us today, we will find other ways of getting to her. There's not that much to do here. I think at the moment, we're the only guests." Eden grabbed her purse and opened the ill repaired door. "Let's get this show on the road."

Jerry Anderson ardently watched as the Explorer slowly bumped and jerked down the rough gravel road, never once letting it escape from his intense stare. He watched until it was no longer in his range of sight, standing patiently for two minutes more, just to make sure the women were well on their way. Then he took the ring of keys from the drawer behind the reception desk and walked to the door. He hesitated for a second, smiled, and turned around. He went behind the bar and retrieved an old dented toolbox.

He mumbled out loud into the empty lodge room. "I have to cover all my bases. After all, I am the owner and repairs have to be made. No better time than the present." He laughed, which displayed his slightly uneven teeth. "Those bitches think they can play games with me? We'll see about that."

The yellow gravel of the driveway crunched under his feet as he made his way to the cabin to the right of the drive. He turned around one more time, squinted his eyes as he looked toward the road. There was barely enough light in the room to see clearly. He didn't risk turning on the overhead light fixture. He walked into the bathroom to look for anything. Maybe pill bottles, he thought. There would be names on medicine bottles. There was nothing on the vanity besides the obvious wet toothbrushes and curling iron. One of the pieces of luggage was on the bed by the window. It was open, a good place to begin. He carefully reached into to side pouch, nothing. Then he boldly began to take out the clothes. What's the point?, he thought. I should be looking for letters or printed material if I am going to discover the idenity of these illusive strangers. He jumped when he heard a vehicle on the loud gravel driveway. "Oh, shit." He said out loud. He grabbed his metal toolbox and walked through the door onto the cement door stoop.

"Did I catch you doing some work?" Chris Bagley, the mailman, waved and continued into the lodge with his parcel of junk mail.

Jerry went back into the cabin, more determined than ever to find something. They're not that smart. How could they have taken every solitary clue? That's when he separated some sweaters in one of the suitcases, revealing an envelope. It was not sealed. He became excited, the edges of his lips turned up. Finally, he thought, we will know who you are and why you are here.

Jerry Anderson's hands visably shook with anticipation as he opened the white envelope. A neatly folded piece of white paper greeted him. Carefully, he unfolded it and began to read the bold hand printing on the letter. It said: Got ya. How stupid do you think we are, Jerry?

His lips grew tight, and his nostrils flared in rage. "We'll see, you little whores. You may think that you've won the battle, but you haven't won the war. Far from it."

The Explorer sped toward Bear Junction. The stress seemed to have left Phyllis' face. "I am so glad that Jerry let me leave with you. This should be fun, but I can't be gone too long. He wants me back by two."

Eden gritted her teeth at that last comment, but she kept silent. She decided that it was a good idea to simply concentrate on the scenery. "The woods are so dark and deep. This must be a dismal place in the winter months." She wondered if the views would be more pleasing to the eye if they weren't here for such ominous reasons.

"You're absolutely right. It's far worse in the winter. It is beautiful with the snow and pine trees, but it is so quiet, cold, and desolate. Even the birds have enough sense to leave."

"Are you happy up here, Phyllis?" Melissa never minced many words.

"Why would you think that life had anything, whatsoever, to do with happiness?"

Nancy didn't want to ruin her chances by too much too soon. "Look, what's that?"

"A deer and her fawn. You see a lot of that this time of year. You've got your camera. Do you want to stop and take a picture?"

Eden obliged and took the camera, carefully getting out of the vehicle. She aimed the camera and pretended to take the picture, not actually clicking. Photos are evidence, she thought.

They were still outside of Bear Junction when Phyllis directed Eden to turn down a deserted road. "There is a wonderful little antique shop about two miles on the left. It's especially wonderful because the tourists don't know about it. That keeps the prices from skyrocketing."

It was a farmhouse with a little shed about fifty feet away. It had a sign that looked unprofessionally painted. Junk and Stuff was painted in red on a sign.

Nancy laughed. "Not much pride in their product."

A chubby older woman with a golden retreiver came out of the house and greeted them as they descended from the Explorer. She was wiping her hands on a tea towel.

"Beautiful day for antique shopping."

"It's a beautiful day for anything, Martha."

"Phyllis, I never see you anymore. This is such a treat." The lady smiled and embraced Phyllis in a warm way. Her body looked like massive goose down pillows tied up with a faded flowered apron. "Don't tell me that you're so busy over there that you can't spare a minute for a visit with an old friend and have a cup of coffee."

"It's not that. You know Jerry. He doesn't like me to be gone."

"How did you manage to get out today?"

"These are our guests from Wilderness Lodge. They don't know their way around, plus I promised to pick up groceries on the way back. But, come to think of it, he didn't make much of a fuss. Strange, I expected a fight."

Melissa couldn't help sneaking a smile in the direction of Nancy. Melissa spoke to Nancy in a quiet voice. "She looks ten years younger when she's away from that bastard."

Martha produced a key to the shop. Nancy thought it was a renovated chicken coup. It was small and cluttered, with dusty furniture, small objects and old books piled everywhere. Nancy closed her eyes for a moment and imagined that she could still smell the aroma of chicken droppings. What a turn her life had taken in just a few days. There would be no returning to the way it was. She thought, in a week it will be over. But, will it ever really be over?

Melissa and Nancy could hardly take their eyes off Eden. They both found it difficult to control their laughter so they decided that it would be wise not to look at each other. Eden was obviously repulsed by the junk in the coup. Martha was trying to convince her that an orange ceramic lamp, circa 1950, was a wonderful find. They both wondered how long Eden would be content to control her mouth.

"As lovely as the lamp is, I'm looking for older objects. Maybe Victorian or Queen Ann." The smell affected Eden, her eyes began to water. Then she started to sneeze and cough. Melissa swiftly took her under her elbow and guided her out into the fresh air.

"Now that was fun." To add insult to injury, the yellow dog showed his teeth and growled.

Martha was mortified by the nasty dog's behavior. "Shep, stop that, this instant. I don't understand. He is usually such a nice dog. I have never seen him act like this."

Eden fought to catch her breath. "Animals and men always react to me in the same way. I always say that going to a club and going to the zoo is about the same." She laughed, but found this experience unsettling.

The two old chairs that sat next to the building allowed her an opportunity to compose herself. Melissa, Phyllis and Martha chatted next to the Explorer."Nancy, I might need one of your pills to calm my nerves."

"I left them in Rockton. I knew that I would never need them again."

Eden rubbed Nancy's arm. "Have I ever told you how proud I am of you?"

"Eden, my definition of freedom is not to let your past affect your today."

Melissa climbed into the drivers seat. "Let's get going. Beth, you are definitely in no condition to drive, so I'm taking over."

Eden apologized to Martha, and the women continued on their journey. Phyllis explained that the shop was a converted chicken coup. That was the reason for Eden's coughing attack. She said that many people are allergic to chickens.

Bear Junction was larger than they remembered from that rainy night. "There's Carl's Place. We stopped there for a drink and a dance." Melissa turned to look at Eden, who solomonly shook her head.

"Phyllis, what is there to do here?" Nancy pointed to a farmers market in a roped off area across from Carl's Place. "Let's walk through there."

The friends laughed and talked. When they finally finished, each of them was carrying a bag of fresh produce. Eden's plan was working, Phyllis Anderson was growing closer and closer to them. Oddly enough, they were growing closer to her, as well.

At one point, Nancy and Phyllis were engaged in a private conversation. Eden pulled Melissa aside. "Try to contrive a way to separate ourselves from Nancy and Phyllis. It would be to our advantage to let Phyllis confide in her. Any ideas?"

Melissa absentmindedly ran her fingers across her forehead. "One more frigging antique shop and then I'll suggest that we split up."

"What excuse will you give?"

"Who knows, I'll think of something. Leave it to me. I wasn't married three times for nothing."

THIRTEEN

Eden pointed to a fairly respectable antique shop. "How about that one?"

Nancy wrinkled her nose. "I'm sick to death of that musty old crap. Enough already. Phyllis, why don't you and I fend for ourselves? Let's leave Marcy and Beth to their own devices."

"Maybe while they go through the shops, we could have lunch and grocery shop."

"Great, we will meet you back here in two hours sharp. Ann, take the keys so you can load the groceries." Eden discreetly winked at Melissa as Nancy and Phyllis climbed into the Explorer.

"Thank God, I can take this wig off, I'm sweating like a pig." Melissa began to lift the front of the straight brown wig off her head, sweat beads on her forehead glistening in the warm sun.

"Stop, you can't do that. One minuscule mistake could blow us right out of the water. We've become almost famous in this idiotic little town. Leave it on, you know that we can't risk having anyone see you as a red head. Melissa, we are all we have. We are like three sisters who need to love and support each other. We're in the middle of a war zone, trying to be brave but none of us know where this is going to take us. By the way, I agree with you. Jerry Anderson is not worthy of one minute in prison for any of us. You have never really voiced your true thoughts on this."

"I don't know, honestly. My life wasn't wonderful before this trip. The only thing I know for sure is that I need to come to some ending with this fear and hate I feel for this man. Keep in mind that we are the only ones who can give him the power to destroy our lives."

Eden and Melissa walked into a small park in the center of town. They sat on a wooden park bench and let the sun warm their faces. Melissa chose the shaded side of the bench. "What do you think Nancy and Phyllis are talking about?"

Eden thought for a brief moment before she answered. "This is just the beginning. Hopefully, Phyllis is commiserating about the monster she's married to. Nancy is a terrifically sensitive person. She will know just how hard to push and exactly when to stop. I do think there is more to Phyllis than meets the eye. I really wanted to hate Jerry Anderson's wife; life would have been much simpler. It just made sense that she would be evil. But, instead I feel sorry for her and would really like to save her. We have to be patient and realize that everything doesn't have to be accomplished in one day."

"Do you think Jerry Anderson has any regrets or conscience?"

"No, he's a sociopath. A sociopath can justify anything he has ever done. But I also believe that he dug his own grave. He is the most miserable man I have ever met."

Eden closed her eyes and let the soft breeze wash over her body. She was wearing a pair of navy blue walking shorts and a light blue tee shirt. The cool wind felt good on her bare legs.

"Have you ever forced yourself to go to a party that you dreaded, and then it turned out to be one of the most memorable experiences of your life. I feel as though this is one of those parties. This particular party is going to change all of our lives. We are going to leave it different people than who came to it."

"Nobody is all good or all bad, but I feel that Jerry Anderson is evil. Eden, I know I'm no philosopher. I am a realist, so I am so grateful that you remembered your revolver. I believe in my heart of hearts that that man is capable of anything. If he could molest little girls, he could commit murder. He already attempted to murder our souls."

"Men like Bob and Jerry Anderson are cowards. Neither of them would take on a real man. They prey on the defenseless. How little they know. The three of us have an endless supply of strength and fortitude, and they will soon discover that fact. Melissa, you can be sure that we will be the winners. If nothing else comes out of this experience, maybe we can all get off the guilt treadmill."

"Why don't we walk through that antique shop and

then try to find someplace for lunch? We better make sure that it isn't the same place that Nancy and Phyllis are eating. They really need time together. Thank God for Nancy, I don't think either one of us could pull it off."

Nancy saw a drug store and pulled the Explorer to the curb. "I forgot conditioner, do you mind?"

"Of course not, Ann, but you could kill two birds and buy it in the supermarket."

"I'm pretty fussy about what I put on my hair." Nancy lied. "I'll treat to lunch if you can direct us to a nice place." Nancy grabbed some toothpaste and conditioner and slipped her Visa out of her billfold and then put it back into her purse. "I think I'll pay cash instead."

"There are not too many fancy restaurants in Bear Junction. If you want to drive ten minutes, I know a cute little tearoom that is part of a high-end bed and breakfast. I don't expect you to treat, I put some money aside. Jerry doesn't even have to know. But, if he asks please tell him that you paid."

Nancy laughed and shook her head. "Trust me, I know exactly what you are talking about. You didn't put it into a teapot by any chance?"

"What are you talking about?"

"I didn't use my teapot for tea. It was used as my own private little bank for money that I ended up calling my escape fund. I had enough for a long time and still didn't have enough nerve to use it. I am so void of even a small grain of self esteem that it left me with no courage."

"What made you take the money out of your teapot and leave? Where did you get the nerve? I'm sorry I don't mean to pry. Feel free not to answer me if it makes you feel uncomfortable. I don't have any right to ask you to tell me your personal business."

"I realize that you don't know me very well, yet. But, I feel a deep connection with you, Phyllis. I don't feel uncomfortable talking to you. I sense the only difference between us is our age. You are just an older version of who I was."

"Exactly, Ann, it wasn't too late for you. Tell me what pushed you over the edge. Please tell me what made you open the lid of your teapot."

"The money was still in the teapot until last Friday morning. That's when I left for good. There will be no going back. I lived in a cold black box for so many years, and it feels so good to be finally out. I feel like a four-year-old."

"You have two wonderful friends for support. You are so much more fortunate than most women."

"Phyllis, are we talking about most women or are we talking about you specifically?" Nancy took a deep breath as she wondered if she said too much and pushed Phyllis too far.

They pulled the Explorer into the parking lot of Betty's Bed and Breakfast and Tearoom. It provided an opportunity to pause the heavy conversation, giving Phyllis a reason not to answer Nancy's question. Betty's was a remarkable Victorian mansion painted peach. The trim sported several different colors, including blue and cocoa brown. Nancy thought it was one of the most beautiful houses that she had ever seen. Betty greeted them when they walked in the unusual but ancient stained glass front door. She looked a lot like her mother-in-law, Doris. They were seated in a room among several round tables with table clothes that reached to the floor. The long narrow windows were dressed in lace curtains that were tied back with pink silk rose buds and ribbons. The walls were adorned with flowered wallpaper.

"There is only one word to describe this place, charming."

Betty smiled and thanked Nancy for her kind words. She seated them by the window that looked out into a formal English garden, complete with a cherub fountain. The window was open just enough so they could hear the water and birds chirping.

"Phyllis, let's eat slowly. The longer we can stay her, the better."

Betty brought tea and tiny bone china cups. "We don't use menus here. Everyday is different. It hinges completely on my mood and what I want to cook. In fact, some days I don't cook at all. On one of those days, our specialty is tea sandwiches."

Phyllis looked surprised. "Please tell me that is the

case today. What fun to have an English high tea."

Betty laughed. "No, my dear, it isn't the case today. But who says that we can't make it the case? If you want an English high tea, you will have it."

When Betty left their table, Phyllis apologized. "I am so sorry, you might have wanted something else. I was so thoughtless."

"I want to have an agreement with you. No more apologies. Besides, who else would be having a formal English tea in Bear Junction, Wisconsin? This will have to be an experience that will go with me into the nursing home."

Phyllis smiled. "How can you keep your wonderful sense of humor after all you have just gone through?"

Nancy reached across the small round table and gently patted Phyllis' hand. "Phyllis, it's easy. It's much easier now than it was when I was so on edge and frightened of every one of Bob's words and moods."

"That's the first time you used his name. I know that Ann is not your real name. Is Bob his correct name?"

"Yes, it is. But let this be our little secret. I am not quite ready to confront him yet. And, there is another reason, as well, why I want to stay anonymous. I promise you, on my word of honor, that when the time is right, you will know who I am."

The brass bells on the front door chimed as two plump elderly ladies walked into Betty's. They were dressed to the nines, complete with large flowered hats.

Nancy looked up from her cup of tea. "The one in the pink suit is so cute, listen to her voice. She sounds like a pigeon. Phyllis, we could be in Victorian London. I just love this place. You and I both deserve to have some joy in our lives. I just wish that you could be as happy as I am."

"What do you mean? I love it here, too."

"I don't mean just for the moment. I'm not talking about Betty's Tearoom, I'm referring to the rest of your life."

"You're young, you have so much to look forward to, but sometimes we get on a path that we can't leave."

"Every path has an exit. Trust me, Phyllis; you are talking to somebody who thought like you, not too long ago. And, might I add, it's never too late. I'm living proof. Let's change the subject. Did you have a career before you got married?"

"Yes, I was a legal secretary. And, a good one, I might add. I worked for several years for a Rockford attorney. When we moved to a small town, I worked for a country lawyer until he retired. My mind was always working. That life was so long ago but I still remember how fulfilling it was. Jerry hasn't let me work for quite a few years. I think we all need to be needed, don't you?"

"Needed or possessed? Sometimes there's an invisible line between the two." Betty brought a three-tiered serving tray piled with wonderfully delectable treats. "I'm so glad that you offered this as one of our options, it looks like a picture."

The top plate had desserts, complete with tarts, chocolate dipped strawberries, shortbread cookies, and pastry. The second had tiny crustless white bread sandwiches. They were made with cream cheese and cucumbers. The third had dark bread ham and cheese sandwiches. Nancy thought the atmosphere was perfect for delving into Phyllis' head and with a small bit of finesse, it would happen. Nancy was well aware that the success of their plan hinged completely on her communication skills.

FOURTEEN

O h, my God, I think I have totally taken leave of my senses. Can you believe that I had enough nerve to order meat loaf in this scummy diner?" Eden wrinkled her nose and poked at the mushy mess on her plate with the tip of her knife.

Melissa seemed delighted. "And you're the smart one?"

"Do you want to trade?"

"Hell, no. Sometimes we have to take responsibility for our bad choices. Besides, my sandwich doesn't look nearly as disgusting."

"I can hardly wait to get Nancy alone. What do you think she found out?"

"Probably what we already know. That Jerry is a piece of shit. We know that he is abusive with Phyllis' mind. I wonder if he beats her too."

"I doubt if Phyllis will admit anything like that to Nancy. After all, just yesterday they were strangers to each other."

"Eden, you were gone for a long time. I'm going to tell something about Nancy. She has more strength than you can even imagine. Please, don't mistake her kindness for weakness. I know she will come back with more information than we'll even know what to do with. Another thing, she has an awesome memory, remember how smart she was in school? There won't be much that she'll forget. You told me to be patient. This is only our first day. So what, if we don't make much headway. Like Scarlet says, 'tomorrow's another day'. Don't expect too much, Nancy might be taking it slow and just laying a foundation."

"I think this meatloaf is Wisconsin road kill."

"Suck it up. Be a good girl and eat your packaged mashed potatoes and canned gravy. Here, take half my sandwich. I was looking for an excuse to order a piece of cherry pie anyway." Melissa picked up half of her sandwich and put it on the edge of Eden's plate. "I said earlier that I was relieved that you carried that revolver in your purse. Tell me that you aren't going to kill him."

"I made you and Nancy a promise. Whatever happens will be a decision among the three of us, and I meant it. I am not going to let loose of that gun. It stays with us. We all know that Jerry Anderson is a nut case. He has already proven that. But let's not forget that he's a big man, at least in stature, definitely not in character. That gun will be used for self-defense only unless we decide to the contrary. At this point, the gun will only be used for protection. I've got another point that I want to make with both of you. We all need to promise each other that we will stay close. I don't want any of us to be alone with him under any circumstance. So far, it has been soft and sweet, but you know that we will, eventually, have to confront the devil."

"Finish up, I want to get out of here and go antique shopping."

"Antique shopping? You hate antiques. We don't

have transportation so let's just walk up and down the street and see what stores are open. Today is Sunday and this is a small town. The most exciting place in Bear Junction might be the supermarket."

"The antique store has an open sign on it, let's go."

Eden paid the bill with cash, under protest from Melissa. "Save your money, I've got plenty. When I run out, we can start on yours. I don't want to waste time thinking about unimportant issues."

"Money is important, Eden. So many times in my life, money was difference between eating and not eating."

"It isn't to me, but I'm sorry for hitting a nerve, Melissa. This antique store isn't at all impressive from the outside." Eden made that comment as they walked through the simple front door. It was a strange shop, narrow and long. There seemed to be no end to its length. "It's very dark in here." Eden squinted to see to the far end of the store. Most of the light came from an undersized window at the front, next to the entry.

"There doesn't seem to be anyone here."

Melissa walked down three wood stairs, making her way toward the back. Besides the colorful old Oriental carpets that were placed strategically around the store, the store exhibited only hard wood floors. Eden's interest was wholly consumed by a mirror. She was so enthralled that she was not aware of talking quietly to herself.

She thought that Melissa was standing close behind her. "I've never seen anything like it. It is so beautiful with all the gold leafing and carving. It must be old, but where could it have come from? I don't know anybody who has a house with ceilings high enough to accommodate it. It has to be thirteen feet high, at least." Eden wondered if it was salvaged from an elegant old hotel lobby or museum. She found herself awestruck with its beauty. She gently ran her fingers over the intricate carving, almost seductively.

The voice behid her was not of Melissa, it was a strong masculine voice. "Leave it to a Scorpio to be fascinated with that mirror."

"I'm not a Scorpio." Eden lied to the man who appeared to be out of place in this obscure shop. She tried to relax a little, until noticing that he had an uncanny resemblance to Orson Wells. The hair stood up in the back of her neck. She didn't believe in ghosts or the supernatural. That was just fodder for fairy tales. The shop, like its unusual proprietor, was neat, large and immaculate. It was appropriately filled with interesting and well cared for antiques, not junk. In his own right, he was not attractive, but definitely demanded a certain presence. She looked down at his shoes, wondering where he found the ridiculously outdated style. Maybe they're European, she thought. His age was impossible to estimate. He was heavy and well dressed. His suit was formal and old world, something like seen in an old English film. He wore a vest and watch fob. His hair was salt and pepper and neatly slicked back from his face. She wondered if the strange man could hear her heart pounding. She had the urge to run away, but morose curiosity kept her glued to the old wooden floor.

Melissa wandered through the shop, innocently out of touch with what was transpiring between Eden and the strange man.

"Of course you're a Scorpio. Please don't try to talk your way clear of that pride of yours. Just relax and listen to the information that I have for you. I will give you the honor of telling you something else. This journey to Bear Junction is the most important journey of your life. You will take something from here that will change you forever. Don't look to replace your pain for happiness. Earth is a schoolhouse and some of the lessons you learn aren't necessarily pleasant. I have a message for you. If you think you are not ready, I suggest that you climb into your vehicle and leave quickly, not ever to look back."

Although the shop was immaculate, the narrow ray of light that shown through the window reflected the dust that was in the air. As she shifted her position, Eden felt pockets of cold. The hair stood up on the back of her neck.

Melissa walked up behind them with a green painted vase. "How much do you want for this?"

He looked at her, said nothing, and walked slowly through the store and sat down at an impressive hand carved desk at the back.

"Melissa, I need to leave here."

"But I want to buy this vase. I don't think he heard me. What language was he speaking? I don't speak French. It sounded like French."

"I said that I need to leave." Eden's voice was firm.

When the two women stood on the sidewalk in front of the store, Melissa spoke. "What was that all about? Did he make a pass at you?"

"No, nothing like that, I don't know. I can't seem to talk about it right now. I need to compute what just happened and maybe we can discuss it later."

"Hey, there's Nancy and Phyllis." Melissa hurried to the side of the street and pretended she was hitchhiking.

Eden said under her breath. "Sometimes Melissa's short attention span works to everybody's benefit."

Nancy stopped to pick up her two friends. "I noticed that you've bought the groceries."

Nancy smiled. "That wasn't the highlight of our day. We were doing more important things, like eating in the most marvelous Victorian mansion. Phyllis and I had a high English tea, complete with scones, strawberries and cream. It was an event for all our senses."

Eden was mute on the way back to Wilderness Lodge. She contemplated many things. She was not so absorbed in the antique store experience, however, that she was insensitive to the ambiance inside the Explorer. There was, now, a definite keen connection between Nancy and Phyllis. The time they spent together was unquestionably the defining factor.

Melissa thought that the drive from Bear Junction to Wilderness Lodge took forever. She could hardly wait to get Nancy alone to hear how the conversation went. She tried to think of how she could get a hint but decided that she best not appear obvious.

After they helped Phyllis unload the groceries into the stuffy antiquated kitchen, Eden suggested that they take a walk along the shore of Lake Superior. The Lodge was only about two hundred feet from the shoreline.

Eden hoped that Phyllis wouldn't want to go with them, but she felt obligated to ask. "Come with us, Phyllis."

"No, we got back late, and I haven't even thought about dinner. Will you be eating here or going back to town? I'll do something simple, maybe pork chops, mashed potatoes and veggies."

Melissa blurted. "Definitely here. And I'm sure Beth will agree. Our lunch wasn't exactly a culinary delight." God, she thought, how she hated trying to remember everybody's bogus names.

"If you are going to walk along the shore, use your repellent and watch for bears. Don't go too far. I don't want to lose my new best friends to bears, bugs, or those vicious wild squirrels."

Eden secretly enjoyed the teasing, although she would be damned if she let them know it. It had been a long time since she had friends who cared enough to tease her. So much of her life had been devoted to business cronies. She reached into her purse and found the repellent. Then they walked down the steep embankment, through patches of weeds and large rounded rocks until they got to the water. The gentle waves lapped the shore like a mother cat bathing her kitten.

Melissa took off her shoes and put her warm feet into the cold wet sand. "Okay, out with it. What did you learn from Phyllis?"

"Twenty more years with Bob and I would have been Phyllis. She is a delightfully sensitive woman who is trapped in a horrific marriage. Do you know she is a legal secretary?"

Eden ignored her last comment and only wanted the facts. "Did you make any headway? Did she admit to being abused?"

"Eden, be patient. Phyllis trusts me, that's pretty easy to see. She has it even worse than I did. She thinks that she is too old to make a change. She told me that I was lucky to have such good friends to help me. I told her that I wanted to be her friend, but it was too soon. She wouldn't really open up totally. She listened while I volunteered info about Bob and me. It's going to take awhile."

"Did she talk about her daughter in Texas?"

"I tried to, but it was painful for her to talk about her.

She did say that she was a rebellious kid. At one point she ran away having problems with boys and drugs. Phyllis said that she finally straighted herself out. Maybe not straightened herself out, she got straightened out with lots of detention and therapy. I wanted to ask her how Jerry behaved with his daughter, but I could feel her began to clam up. Not to make excuses, but I think I did damn good. If I go gangbusters on this, she is going to avoid me like the plague. Keep in mind, Phyllis Anderson is not a stupid woman."

"I say we back off a little bit. We don't have to be in her face all the time. We've really done well for the short amount of time we've been here. If we start getting impatient, we're going to back slide."

"You're right, Melissa. Let's have a quiet pork chop meal at the lodge tonight and minimal contact with Jerry. We can start again in the morning. The worst thing we could possibly do is to make her suspicious. Or worse yet, make Jerry suspicious. Nancy, do you think Jerry physically abuses her?"

"Yes. I could tell by the way she avoided that subject. She is beyond doubt frightened of him. That monster has totally depleted her of any grain of self worth. If I ever had any doubts about leaving Bob, this has reinforced my positive decision. Besides, we could entertain ourselves tonight by listening to his messages on the cell phone. Good old Bob, always there for a laugh."

"Another thing we can do when we get back to our humble abode is check to see if Jerry invaded our space. I'm anxious to know if he read our letter."

"How will you know for sure?"

"Melissa took care of that problem. She laid a thread right next to the luggage. If he opened the top, it would have moved it slightly. Bam, we've got our answer. Leave it to Melissa to figure that out."

Melissa dramatically flicked her hand into the air. "Hey, I was married three times, what can I say?"

FIFTEEN

They walked for about an hour or so along the shoreline. A certain late afternoon light reflected off the water. Melissa took a deep breath and could smell the strong aroma of pine. "I want to get back to the cabin and shower before dinner. I have to admit, I am more than curious to find out if Jerry Anderson was sniffing around in our room."

"Let's take it slow and easy tonight at dinner. I think that it's still too early to have any major confrontations with Jerry. Nancy made a lot of inroads today with Phyllis, but we still have a long way to go." Eden tried to sound matter-of-fact.

Melissa stopped her stride. "It sounds like you've cooked-up a plan."

Eden laughed. "Yes, I do have a plan and it's well thought out, not that you two have given me much time to think. Tonight we are going to express an extremely strong interest in boating for tomorrow."

Melissa turned her eyes toward the sky. "Great."

"Hear me out. Believe it or not, I know something about motors. I can cripple that boat's engine without the slightest evidence of tampering. Remember yesterday when I made that quick stop at the hardware store? I bought pliers and a screwdriver. Trust me, that's all I need to get the job done. After dinner, we'll head for our cabin and turn out the lights about a half hour after we arrive, just in case Jerry is keeping track of us. Then we'll sneak down to the pier. I'll disable the motor, and the jackass will spend the whole day tomorrow trying to fix it. Part of his motor will be swimming with the fish at the bottom of the lake. We'll bury the pliers and screwdriver in the woods to get rid of our evidence. In the meantime, Jerry will be too busy to notice that Phyllis is spending so much time with Nancy."

"Honey, you're a genius." Melissa couldn't control herself, jumping up and down in apparent delight.

"Melissa, while Nancy and Phyllis are together tomorrow, I want you to do something for me. Please, come with me to that antique shop, just one more time."

"That strange guy seemed to upset you. Are you obsessed with that place? Why the hell would you even think about going back there?"

"I have so many questions. I need to talk with him. I really need you to go with me. This is something I have to do."

A stubborn look took over Melissa's face. "You are going to have to negotiate that with me. I will go with you on one condition. You have to tell me what that odd man said to make this such a big deal. You are always so secretive and private. You need to tell me what he said, or I don't go. Keep in mind that I won't be any help, because I don't speak a word of French."

Eden was not used to being pushed. She was always the person who did the negotiating. "Okay. I'm not getting into that French bit because I don't speak French either. Let's just agree to disagree about that. He told me to leave right now if I wasn't ready for some huge catastrophic event to happen to me personally. He told me that it was coming soon, and that if I didn't think I could handle the backlash, I should get in the car and high tail it out of Dodge. I need more details. I have to talk to him one more time."

"That guy doesn't have a clue what's going on in our lives. What makes you think he isn't a nut who was just trying to hit on you?"

"Listen, Melissa, we both know that's not true. That comment borderlined on being insulting. Just remember, we're on the same team. I am paid a huge salary to be a good judge of character. That's what I do for a living and I'm damned good at it, Melissa, don't underestimate my skills. I can't be tricked. I know when people are telling the truth, I know when they are genuine, and I can always tell if they are scamming. I'm like a human lie detector. That man had something to say, and it was paramount to my well-being. Are you going to go back to Bear Junction with me and try to find him or not? Give me a simple answer, please."

"Okay, you've got it. But let this be the end of it. It's starting to weird me out."

Nancy had never seen Eden so vulnerable. She looked desperate and it worried her. "What antique shop? What are you two talking about?"

Eden shielded her eyes against the sun as she looked down the shore. "Melissa, tell Nancy all about it on your way back to the cabin. I do my best thinking alone. I hope you two don't mind if I have some down time. Besides, wearing my jogging shoes reminded me about how lazy I've been about running. I usually run fifteen miles on the weekends. I need this time alone to think. Maybe the fresh air and the solitude will give me some outstanding ideas. I'm kind of a loner at heart. This togetherness is making me a little crazy, time alone will clear the cobwebs. I promise I'll meet you two back at the cabin in an hour." Eden looked at her watch.

Nancy affectionately patted Eden's arm. "Are you sure? Let me take your stuff back with us so you don't have to carry anything while you run. Make sure you've got your cell phone."

Melissa filled Nancy in on the antique store details on their way back to the shabby cabin. When they stepped inside, Melissa ran to her bed. "Look, the arrogant idiot didn't even have the good sense to fasten the latch on my luggage. It's almost like he wanted us to know he was in here. It makes my skin crawl knowing that old fart was fondling my underwear."

"Relax, you're way too old for his sick, perverted

tastes. But I do feel like disinfecting my clothes, anyway." Nancy playfully held up one of her shirts with two fingers and made a face. She walked to the window and pulled the frayed curtains closed. "Should we make a few secret inuendos tonight at the lodge?" She sat back down on the edge of her bed. "Phyllis told me she has a special place where she has been hoarding money just like I did. She didn't tell me how much she had though. Remember the deal, none of us will spend even one minute alone with that demon. We are going to stick together like glue, especially now that he knows that we're on to him. That note must have made him crazy. Hopefully it didn't push him over the edge."

Melissa was on her back on top of the bed with her eyes closed "At least we've got each other. Poor Phyllis has nobody."

"Not true, she has us now. But you're right, after we leave she will have nobody. I hope in the short time we're here, I'll be able to convince her to take her life back."

"Okay, now for the entertainment. Nancy, get out your cell phone and check your messages." Melissa tossed Nancy her purse.

Nancy obliged by dialing a couple of numbers and listening. "It seems there are six messages." She sat silent and sober for at least fifteen minutes, quietly concentrating. "He would like to kill me. He has been to Eden's house and finally got it through his head that we're not there. He is claiming that his mother, Doris, is ill. Now, he's threatening to sell the house and keep the profits. We knew that he'd close the Visa account, but he found out that I emptied half of the savings. Oh, by the way, I won't have any clothes to come home to because he destroyed them all."

"Don't worry about the house. That should be the least of your problems. I know as a fact that he can't sell it without your signature at closing. Even he is smart enough to know that. Bob's just blowing hot air." Melissa left her prone position to sit next to Nancy on her bed. She could feel her trembling. "Honey, you're not having any regrets, are you?"

Nancy would have sighed if she weren't so determined to appear strong. "Yes, I am, as a matter of fact. I regret not doing this twenty years ago. This is a week of cleansing for me."

"Do you think that old bag is really sick, or it is one of Bob's ploys to get you back? Two of his favorite tactics are shame and guilt. How are you going to deal with it?"

"If it is true, it's about time that Bob dealt with his own mother. I have been the caregiver all these years. I was their prisoner, and I say, 'No more'. They can work out their own problems any way they see fit. I am gone, I am really gone. No one will ever control me again."

"Are you ever going to listen to the rantings of his messages again?"

"Of course, I will. I'd be a fool not to. He gets so hysterical that he gives away all his evil plots. Bob has no control over his mouth when he's in a rage. As soon as I get back to civilization, I will have Eden help me find the best lawyer in Illinois. She probably knows a dozen of them."

"Bravo. Like I say every day, Nancy, I am so proud of you."

"Any ideas about how we're going to handle Phyllis tomorrow? I'm sure Jerry won't let her leave again. God forbid, not two days in a row. The only reason he let her go today was so he could search our room. I hope Eden doesn't get carried away with her running and forgets the time. I can't wait to tell her about Jerry digging through our stuff."

SIXTEEN

Eden watched her friends fade into the distance. She noticed that the air had dropped in temperature several degrees and the gentle breeze was becoming more aggressive as it pushed her hair away from her forehead. This is perfect weather for a good refreshing run, an hour would work quite well. Running along the shore of a Great Lake was not new to Eden, she ran most every weekend on the shores of Lake Michigan. She took one more look at her watch and decided that she would run twenty minutes up the shore and twenty minutes back. That way she could sit and relax for ten minutes before heading back to the cabin. The only sounds she could hear was the waves, the gulls, and the sucking sound of her soles in the damp rocky sand. The wet shoreline gave enough firmness under her shoes to be able to gather some speed. It felt so good to be running again. At last, she felt liberated and in control.

She reached into her pocket when her cell phone began to ring. She said out loud, "I thought I turned that damned thing off."

"Yes, hello, Justin. Talk fast, my battery is about to go dead." She heard a beep and then her premonition was realized. Eden laughed out loud as she slid the sleek silver phone back into her pocket. She knew she had to charge it, but it just didn't seem too important.

"Tomorrow is another day." She smiled at her wit and continued to run down the shore.

She tried cleansing her mind of any thoughts. More than anything else, she wanted this time to fully enjoy the brute nature of the northern wilderness. The smells and the sounds should have been enough to keep her mesmerized, but in spite of her stubborn effort, the thoughts sifted in, first slowly and then in a flood. She thought about the antique store first. She knew in her heart of hearts that what that strange man said was life altering and only a fool would dismiss it. Time flew, her twenty minutes evaporated quickly. Eden stood for a moment solely to enjoy the dynamic view of the lake before starting back. She thought fleetingly of encountering a bear, but then decided not to torment herself. She was all too aware of not having her purse and her beautiful shiny revolver. Then in a flash of reality, she remembered that she didn't have a phone either. In case of danger or emergency, she had nothing. She realized that she was as defenseless as a child. That shocking truth made her eyes dart, first left and then right. She took a deep breath and made the decision not to let her fear ruin a perfectly good run. She turned and began her run back. Now the wind was to her back and pushed her hair carelessly into her face. With the sun beginning to set, Eden was relieved to head back to the cabin.

Fifteen minutes into the return, Eden's fears were realized. Jerry Anderson jumped out from behind a large gray boulder that positioned itself close to the edge of the sand. He stood directly in front of her, hands on his hips, sporting an ugly cynical grin displaying his nicotine stained teeth. She couldn't control herself, she screamed loudly. There was nobody within hearing distance, but she screamed instinctively and loudly. Jerry looked at her and laughed in her face. "Scare the shit out of you, little girl? You were never the screamer before. Have your habits changed?"

He grabbed her wrist with such agility and force that it wasn't difficult to force her to the ground. Eden's wrist felt like it was snapping, but she wasn't going to give him the satisfaction of knowing. "I may be petite, but you will soon figure out that I'm way past being that poor defenseless little girl you used to know."

"Your biggest mistake would be to play me for the fool. Don't scream or fight. I'll save you the trouble, because we both know it's useless. You can scream your damn head off and there is nobody to hear you. I'm twice your size and three times your strength. I've been watching you three very closely, like a tiger, waiting for one of you to stray from the herd. Low and behold, my waiting finally paid-off and I caught myself dinner. To be honest, I was hoping it would be one of the others, but I'll take what I can get. Yes, you will do quite nicely."

"If you're going to rape me, get on with it. But, I'm going to warn you about having an unpleasant surprise."

Jerry relaxed his hold on Eden's wrists, but not enough for her to get free. "You can calm down for a minute. I haven't decided exactly what I'm going to do with you. To be honest, you're way too old for my tastes. I like my partners young, sweet, and tender. Most of all I like them untainted. But you already know that, don't you?"

"Partner? Now that's an interesting choice of words. I think you mean, victim. You were never man enough for a real woman. You had to prey on children."

"Shut your God damn mouth." He hit her in the face in his uncontrollable rage. "Now I'm going to talk and you're going to shut up. You don't think that your weak disguises threw me off, did you? That was a funny little joke you left in that envelope in that suitcase. You pissed me off and that just made me look further and more intensely. I found a paper in the pocket of a pair of jeans. I knew who you three were, but I just couldn't put my finger on it. Then I found that receipt with Nancy's name on it and bingo. I've always been one step ahead of you and your two friends. I'm sure you're going to run back to the cabin, that is if I let you, and tell Melissa and Nancy that your cover has been blown."

"Don't assume anything. If you rape me, that's a different story. Then, of course, the law will be involved. If you want to talk, I would consider making this meeting our little secret. I have been waiting for years to confront you. Actually, I have been waiting for years to kill you. I have always dreamed of trading my innocence for your life. It isn't a fair trade, but it's the only one that makes sense. I have lain awake many nights dreaming about how I would make your death the most painful possible."

Jerry laughed, taunting her sincerity. "Why do you think I'm any different than any other man? Every man has that same secret need, I was just fortunate to have the opportunity. Teachers aren't paid much, but I sure took advantage of the perks."

Eden tried not to play into his hand, but that last comment turned her face bright red and her breathing came in short gasps. "Not every man. Just you and other perverts like you. You all should be lined up against a wall and shot, then you can compare notes in hell."

His face was close and his foul breath was about to make her vomit. Wretched memories from the far past came flooding back in waves. Eden kept calm on the outside even though her heart was about ready to leap out of her chest. She learned that trick in negotiations that affected her business life. There was nobody who could read Eden McNeal's face.

"There is nothing that turns my blood to fire like the feel of lovely young soft flesh under my hands. I haven't had that kind of passion for quite a while. Looking at you now, maybe I could imagine and remember what it felt like with you. You're still little, you haven't grown that much. You were a juicy little peach ready to be plucked. Not all little girls mind being looked at as a sexual object."

"Yes, they do. Children are meant to be children, full of innocence and wonder. I was not put on this earth to satiate your sick, perverted pleasures." Eden took advantage of his weakening grip and yanked her wrists free. "My parents were good people who moved to Rockton from Chicago to raise a family. They moved there because it was a safe little village. I wish now that I would have told them. My father would have killed you. If he failed, you would be entertaining Bubba in State Prison."

She sat up, but did not take advantage of this opportunity to get up and run. She knew she could easly outrun him, unless he injured her, but decided that this was the only chance she would have to face her demon. She wanted to rub her wrists to get the circulation flowing again, but resisted. She wouldn't give that bastard the pleasure of knowing that he hurt her.

"I could kill you. These woods never see people. I could bury you in a shallow grave, or not even bury you at all. The animals would have a feast on your sweet tender body. Nobody would be the wiser. Unfortunately, you brought Melissa and Nancy with you. They would send out people to search. Just keep in mind that I am extremely resourceful. I have grown to know this area, and there is no remote place that hasn't escaped me. Ever since we moved here, my eyes have been open for the perfect grave. My dream has always been to use and kill a sweet little girl and put her in a place nobody would ever find, where she would rest peacefully until the end of time, just like a sleeping princess." He sneered. "You're not that young, but you might do nicely in a pinch. After all, it has been a long time."

She decided it was a good idea to ignore his threat, remembering so long ago of how excited he became when she showed fear or cried. "Tell me something. Did you molest your own daughter?" After the words left her mouth, she regretted asking. She knew that that would get him furious.

"That's none of your damn concern. Let's keep this conversation about the business at hand."

"I thought you were proud of your dirty deeds. You said that it was all men's dream to molest children. Why, suddenly are you ashamed? Didn't you just tell me that you were doing what came naturally?"

"My daughter was home grown fruit grown in my own garden. She was there for my taking. Of coarse, I couldn't resist. She belonged to me, I created her. Why shouldn't I take what's mine?" He picked up some of the coarse stony sand and ran it through his hands. His voice dropped. "I know you came here to get even with what you thought was a violation of your childhood, but I would rethink your plan. If I were you, I would definitely postpone telling your whining friends, at least right now. If you relate anything about this meeting, they will run like scared rabbits. I know their habits. You have always been the only one of them with any balls. So, Sweetie Pie, to sum up, if you run back to the cabin and tattle on old Jerry, you will be packing up the Explorer and heading back to Chicago."

His face wasn't as close to Eden's. With the breeze, the stench of his breath no longer turned her stomach. She didn't want to ask, but she was fairly confident that he didn't have a weapon. She was fairly confident that if he did have a weapon, he would have been eager to flaunt it. Her eyes glanced down to the pockets of his pants and she couldn't see anything that looked like a concealed gun or knife. She also noticed that her wrists were beginning to bruise. How was she going to explain that to Melissa and Nancy? This had to be what the man in the antique store was warning her about. She tried to look relaxed as she wondered if this would be the last day of her life. She knew in her heart that Jerry Anderson was more than capable of killing her. If she tried to get up, he would most definitely grab her leg. It was time to create an escape before he overpowered her. Talking with him seemed to get him more and more agitated. Directly behind her and to the right was a fairly large stone, about the size of a man's fist. She rolled her shoulders in a circular direction, to lead him to think that she was trying to relax them. If the stone were just a little bit closer, it would be her chance. Jerry was right about one thing, he was twice her size. She needed to catch him off-guard, she needed to use her head, rather than her strength. All she could think of was to keep him talking. When he was talking, he couldn't think of ways to kill.

"Enough talk. Now I want some action." He clumsily lunged toward her, preparing to grab her wrists once again.

Eden judged that she had only a few seconds, knowing this was the decisive moment, it was do or die. He had already made it quite clear, that in his deranged brain, killing her would be a pleasure. She quickly reached behind her and seized the cold hard stone, making certain that she didn't lose her grip. She brought it forward so fast and forcefully that Jerry didn't know what hit him. He felt the swift terrible pain before he saw the starburst. While he was stunned, Eden jumped to her feet and ran. She ran so hard and long she didn't have a chance to look back. If she had, she would have seen Jerry Anderson lying in the coarse sand with a small trickle of blood coming out of the side of his mouth.

She instinctively knew that he wasn't dead. She couldn't be that lucky. This was going to be a hard secret to keep, but it had to be. Eden hesitated and took two deep breaths before she opened the door to the cabin.

Melissa and Nancy were anxiously waiting for her. Nancy spoke first. "What took you so long? We were about ready to come looking for you."

"I'm sorry. I had an slight accident. I was so busy looking at the lake that I fell over some driftwood. It knocked the wind out of me, so I needed to sit for a few minutes. My phone went dead so I couldn't call you." She smiled and tried to act nonchalant. "Besides, I can run faster than most bears. Well, maybe not. Just Jake."

They sat on the edge of their beds while Nancy and Melissa told her about Jerry's search of the cabin. Eden tried to concentrate and tried even harder to maintain her lie.

SEVENTEEN

Jerry was sitting at his assigned seat at the bar for his usual night's drinking. He didn't even give them the courtesy of a nod, let alone a greeting. Eden wondered if he had a splitting headache, she hoped he did. In reality, she wished that she had killed him. Maybe if she had just turned around and hit him one more time with the rock. She wanted to get a good look at his face to see the damage she administered in the afternoon. But they walked straight back to the kitchen to find Phyllis. She was busy humming as she mashed the potatoes. "I was just thinking about the perfect day I spent in town. I'm going to miss you girls so much."

"We've not gone yet. Let's make the most of it. Do you think we could do something again tomorrow?"

"Umm, maybe not tomorrow, Jerry was in a foul mood when I got back. But I sure had a wonderful time today. I'll never forget it."

"If that boat is available tomorrow, maybe we could take it out on the lake after breakfast. We can't leave here without spending some time on Lake Superior." Eden seemed so sincere that Nancy and Melissa nearly believed her until she turned her head and discreetly winked at them.

"Well, I'm sure it would be all right. You'll need to talk to Jerry about it."

"Let's eat first. Give us the plates, and we'll take them out into the dining area."

They convinced Phyllis to eat with them. All the while Jerry glared at them. After dinner, they went into the bar area and asked him to mix them drinks.

Nancy squinted her eyes in the dim light. "What happened to your face? That's quite a bruise and cut."

"When you work, you have accidents. Not that you women would know anything about work." He poured another drink while he was talking. "I'll tell you something about myself that you probably don't know. I used to be a schoolteacher, in fact, a third grade teacher. I've been missing that. It always gave me pleasure to shape the fragile young mind. So, I decided to get back into it, right here in Bear Junction Elementary School. I have some red tape to go through and some certifications, but all that will soon be resolved. I plan to be a substitute, make a little money. Plus, like I said, I feel the need to shape some fragile young minds."

Melissa said just loud enough for Eden and Nancy's ears. "Ignore him. He's baiting us. Remember what we talked about, be pleasant and brief. Drink up fast and ask him about letting us rent that boat." They clinked their glasses together and Melissa proposed the toast. "Here's to keeping our tongues hooked up to our brains." She gritted her teeth and turned to Jerry Anderson. "Is your boat for hire tomorrow morning?"

"Who wants to know?" He spoke with an edge to his voice.

Eden took charge of the conversation. "I want to know. I'm quite the sailor. Can we rent your boat for tomorrow morning? After breakfast, about ten or so?"

"I don't like getting up too early. Besides, it takes some time to gas it up. How about eleven?"

"I would prefer it a little earlier, but whatever. I guess that would be okay." A slight smile passed Eden's lips. The plan was in motion.

Jerry discreetly walked to the end of the bar where he could whisper to Eden. "I see you took my advice. I guess we'll make this afternoon our little secret." Then his voice became louder for everybody to hear. "How about another drink?"

Nancy said, "Ann has been complaining all day about how tired she is. I think we all feel like turning in early. Thanks anyway. We'll see you tomorrow. None of us fish, so don't get out any fishing gear. We just need some instruction on using the boat."

"Yeah, I've got a feeling you'll need a lot of instruction about how to operate the boat. It's no doubt going to be too much for any of you to handle."

The second they got back to the cabin Melissa chanted in a low guttural voice. "Yea, I've got a feeling you'll need a lot of instruction about how to sail the boat." Melissa swaggered around the room, and all three of the women laughed at her nasty mimicking rendition.

Nancy got serious. "No matter what happens, we can't let that monster to get back into teaching. Everything happens for a reason. We showed up just in time to stop him. We can't knowingly let another child experience what we did. You two have to promise, even if we have to kill him. We can't give that monster the chance to molest one more child."

Melissa rubbed Nancy's shoulders. "Honey, we came to stop him, and stop him we will."

After a half hour, they turned off the cabin lights to appear they were asleep if Jerry were watching. They took a short cut down to the pier, a hard walk in the dark. The slope to the lake was rough with rocks, holes, and weed patches. They thought it was too risky to use the well-worn path. If he were looking out the window, the moon might give them away.

Eden knelt on the wood deck of the boat as Melissa held the flashlight on the motor. Nancy shielded the light by standing in front of it just in case anybody from the lodge would be looking in that direction. The operation took about ten or fifteen minutes and was unquestionably a success.

Melissa said, "Eden, I can't believe you thought of all this today. I spent the whole day with you and didn't have a clue what you were up to."

"I told you that we are a formidable team. Each of us has our strong points, but Nancy is categorically the queen bee."

"Let's make it an early breakfast tomorrow so we can spend even more time with Phyllis before Jerry appears. I have a feeling tomorrow might be it."

Melissa tried to appear innocent by looking wide-eyed. "Please refresh me, I would like to know what "it" is."

"We'd better get out of here before we get caught. We can talk after we get safely inside our cabin." Eden wondered what their reaction would be if she told them about the violent encounter she had with Jerry that afternoon. But, she decided that she wasn't curious enough to tell them. She wouldn't take that risk.

Nancy immediately retrieved her pajamas from her luggage and began to get ready for bed. "Today Phyllis definitely warmed up to me. She knows that my life was not all that different from hers. I feel that this is new to her. She has never had anybody to talk to about it."

"I'm not an idiot. I can see what's going on." Melissa interrupted. "What I want to know is what are we planning to do with all this information? What is the plan? So we know that Jerry is an ass hole. How will that benefit our cause?"

Eden couldn't help but laugh. "Now, Melissa, you are the deep thinker. We're dealing with people, the human mind. Some things can't be analyzed and preplanned. Maybe we should sit here right now and discuss where we think this is taking us. Phyllis Anderson is a direct route to Jerry, that's not even questionable. What is the most important part of Jerry's life? What could we do to screw up his life in the most devastating way? I'm not sure yet. We have only been here a short time. Should we kill him, mutilate him, have him raped by three ugly homosexual men, burn the lodge, or take away Phyllis? I'm no psychic, I guess we'll have to see. What do you think, Nancy?"

"As usual, you seem to make the most sense. I don't know if you really make the most sense, but you are most able to put it into words. I, at least right now, think Phyllis is our only direct line to Jerry. I don't know how valuable she is to him. He might just view her as a replaceable servant. If that's the case, she has no value. No matter what happens I still feel a connection with her. I'll do everything I can to save her. I can't speak for you two, but that's my promise. That's what separates us from animals, the fact that we can feel compassion for other people."

"Eden, don't you think we should stay at the lodge with Nancy tomorrow. I don't feel comfortable going into Bear Junction and leaving her here alone."

"Melissa, you have to understand that Nancy needs to spend time alone with Phyllis. We need to remove ourselves. Plus, she won't be alone. Jerry won't try anything with his wife with anybody else hanging around."

"Eden is right. You two need to leave. Don't worry about me. In fact, if you feel uncomfortable, I'll keep the gun."

"Okay, okay, I'm outnumbered. Speaking of uncomfortable, that antique store experience was weird. I can't understand why you want to go back there. I didn't know you spoke French."

Eden frowned. "French, what are you talking about? I speak Spanish, not French."

"Read my lips, you were speaking French with that odd man at the antique shop. I am 100% sure of it."

"He had an accent, I think, but...."

"I took Spanish in high school, and I'm telling you that you two were speaking French. Why do you think he didn't answer me when I asked him the price of that big green vase? It was because I wasn't speaking French."

"I believe that you think we were speaking French, Melissa, but it makes no sense. Can we just not talk about it any more tonight? I guess we'll have the answer tomorrow when we go back there."

Eden lay awake on her lumpy mattress and stared at the ceiling for what seemed hours after Melissa and Nancy were soundly asleep. She heard every noise of the night, including the beating of her own heart. She recognized the forlorn howling of wolves in the distance. Sometime in the night the wind picked up, which caused branches to scratch across the glass of their small dirty window. Quietly, she got out of bed, so as not to awaken Melissa and Nancy, to double check the lock on the front door. She remembered a movie she saw several years ago, in which wolves broke the window of a cabin and attacked the inhabitants, ripping them to bits. One more time, she got up again and pulled back the curtains to look into the darkness. Eden put her hand down beside her bed. The feel of her leather purse was comforting, especially after her afternoon encounter with Jerry Anderson. She lay on her musty mattress and wondered if keeping that horrible meeting with him a secret was a good idea. After all, her friends did have a right to know how dangerous an adversary he was. Every night she would make sure her revolver was close by, which gave her an immeasurable sense of reassurance. Never again would it be out of her reach. Today's lesson could have been fatal.

Lying in bed quietly, with no conversation, could give her ample opportunity to put her thoughts in rock hard perspective. Her mind ambled back to surreal experience in the antique shop. Could Melissa be right? No, how could French have been spoken? Eden prided herself on her strong, realistic memory. She could recall nothing about the man's speech other than its being articulate and intelligent. It seems there was an accent, but what kind? Should she heed his warning about staying? Jerry Anderson wouldn't be above murder, finding that out the hard way that afternoon. Maybe she should give up this quest and head back to Chicago.

"Eden, it was your idea to get an early start." Melissa was roughly drying her hair with one of the well-worn white bath towels. "'If' we go into town today, I need to buy a couple of towels. God only knows where these have been."

Eden's eyes burned when she tried to open them. "'If is not the proper word. We will be going into town. Remember, you promised that you would go back to that antique shop with me."

"Have you ever forgotten anything in your entire life?"

EIGHTEEN

Now, eight o'clock sharp, they made their exodus from the cabin. The day was several degrees cooler than the day before.

"Thank God it's not as hot as yesterday. That wig about fried my brain." Melissa opened the door to the lodge. "Good, he's not up yet. We'll have some private time with Phyllis."

Phyllis walked from the kitchen, wiping her hands on her faded apron. "I got an early start on breakfast. I knew you'd be here early."

Nancy smiled. "We were seduced by that magnificent aroma of your coffee. I hope you're not going to wait for an invitation this morning, we love your company. Please sit with us and have your breakfast. After all, we won't be spending much time with you today. Hopefully, we will be boating."

"Not for a few hours, Jerry doesn't get such an early start in the mornings. I would expect to be on the water at about eleven."

"That's okay, this isn't the kind of vacation where schedules are very important." Melissa was helping Nancy carry the plates of bacon and eggs to the table.

Eden looked at the food. "I'm going to have to buy a

new wardrobe if I continue to eat these breakfasts."

"I doubt that. That insane energy of yours has always kept you skinny. I, on the other hand...."

Nancy quickly interrupted. "Be quiet you two. It's rude talking about weight when we are about to stuff ourselves with a meal. Besides, it's always the skinny people who talk about weight, fat and calories. Didn't your mother ever teach you manners? What are you going to do today, Phyllis? "Nancy cleverly changed the subject.

"Clean and cook, what else? One day is pretty much like the day before. You girls have been a joy, the high point of my summer." She looked down at her plate in an unsuccessful attempt to disguise the sadness mirrored in her eyes.

"The lake, the trees, the solitude, this could be a wonderful place." Nancy tried to change the subject.

"It could be, but unfortunately...." Her voice trailed off.

Nancy shot Eden a knowing look. "After dinner tonight, let's all watch Letterman. You told me that you enjoy him. We must owe you some money for all the meals that we have been eating here."

"Don't worry about it right now. I'm sure Jerry has it all calculated to the very penny. If it were up to me your visit would be free. You're almost like family, not that Jerry wouldn't blink twice about charging his own family. Although, none of his family speaks to him."

Nancy stood up and affectionately gave Phyllis a hug. "Phyllis, we have no problem with the money. When we came here we realized that we would need to pay for food and lodging. There is more, so much more. I give you my promise that we will sort everything out before I leave this desolate place."

"No, Ann, there is no solution for my problems. You can go home knowing that you made my life a little bit happier."

"Did I see a truck down by the pier this morning?"

"Two men from Milwaukee came yesterday for a few days of fishing. They've been coming every summer for twelve years now. They bring their boat and are usually out on the lake by five. Thank God, I don't have to serve them breakfast. I did pack a lunch for them though. We'll probably be eating fresh lake trout tonight. They love the way I prepare it and they always catch far more than they could ever eat. We kind of inherited them from the old owners. And best of all, they clean their own fish."

"Phyllis, I don't know how you stand it." Nancy narrowed her eyes and gave Melissa a firm look. "Nancy isn't the only person here who has anything in common with you. Phyllis, I want to be your friends as well."

"We are all here for you." Eden watched as Phyllis Anderson gave her a look of puzzlement and surprise. "Things aren't exactly as they seem. And that, my dear lady, is all I am prepared to tell you. At least for now."

"You girls are so mysterious, making me think that your trip to Wilderness Lodge is more than just an innocent vacation for the love of nature."

Melissa laughed. "Just hang in there and don't waste too much time thinking about it. Do you have time for a walk before we leave on our boating adventure?"

"I should get these dishes washed."

Nancy pulled her from her chair. "We'll help. Then we will have an hour or so before the boat's ready. Times a wastin'."

The four women quickly cleaned the kitchen and made their way to the shore of the lake. They walked and they talked, indulging in happy, light conversation. As the three friends earlier decided, the serious talk would only involve Phyllis and Nancy. That was the comfortable, unanimous choice. When they returned, they saw Jerry working on the boat.

In the sunlight he looked even more bloated and colorless. He wore a fishing hat and a sleeveless white tee shirt, which grotesquely called attention to his flabby arms. Melissa turned around and gave Eden a knowing smile. He was kneeling on the pier with his toolbox.

"Ready to go?" Melissa said flatly.

"Hell, no. I can't get this damn thing started. I can't understand why it started fine yesterday and it won't start today." He gave Melissa a dirty look and wiped his filthy hands on the legs of his pants.

Melissa couldn't help but smile. "How long do you think it will be?"

"Do I look like a psychic? How in hell would I know?" He spit the words at her.

Eden grabbed the opportunity. "Who wants to go to Bear Junction with me?"

Melissa raised her hand. "Me, I decided to buy that green vase that I saw yesterday. How about you, Nancy?"

"Thanks, but no thanks. I don't want to go anywhere,

so I'll keep Phyllis company. That is, if she wants my company."

"Of course I do, that goes without saying. It looks like Jerry will be working on that boat for quite a while."

"If he gets that thing working within the next couple hours, give me a call on my cell phone and we'll come right back. Otherwise, we can plan on going boating tomorrow." Eden couldn't help but smile. She knew full well that the boat would need a more accomplished mechanic than Jerry Anderson to get that engine running.

Eden and Melissa turned the Explorer onto the main road and headed toward Bear Junction. "Eden, you look like the cat who swallowed the canary."

"Our plan is working so perfectly, like a well written a script. I really wish Bear Junction wasn't so far."

"What difference? All we have is time in this God forsaken place. Even after we go to the antique store, we'll still have to figure out how to waste more time so that Nancy has enough time with Phyllis. Eden, I'm glad we're going to be alone for a while. We never get a chance to talk. Tell me honestly, how do you really think this is going to pan out?"

"I'm seeing Jerry Anderson in a different light. He's a bitter, unhappy and broken man. When I got here, my favorite fantasy was to see him dead. But, I think he's already dead. Now what?"

"I agree. Isn't our goal to take away his most prized belonging, which would be Phyllis? Then leave him here, stewing in his own juice. That would be the ultimate justice."

"So, what are we going to do after we go to the antique store and shop for your towels? Nancy gave me directions to Betty's Bed and Breakfast. Maybe we could eat lunch there."

Not much was said on the remainder of the drive to Bear Junction. "Eden, slow down and find a place to park. That antique shop is in the next block. What's the name of it?"

"I don't remember seeing a sign with a name on it." Eden parked near the little park in the center of town. "We can stop in that little bath shop and buy some towels on our way back to the Explorer. In fact, I think I'll buy some, too."

"Where is it? Wasn't it on a corner?"

"Yes, it's across the street on the far corner." They crossed the quiet street in the middle of the block and made their way to the front of the antique store. Melissa tried to turn the door handle. It's locked."

They shielded their eyes to be able to see more clearly into the front window, both turning to look at each other at exactly the same moment. A look of alarm mirrored both of their faces. What they saw rendered them speechless. They turned toward the window again in disbelief. The shop was bare. The only recognizable article was the mirror, the large gold leafed mirror that stood alone at the entrance.

"How can that be? There were tons of antiques with no sign of moving-out. No boxes or any clue that this place would be gone this morning. After all, we were here really late in the afternoon, so there couldn't have been nearly enough time to rid this shop of all those antiques."

The lady who ran the flower shop next door put a "'be back soon'" sign in her front window and locked the door to her shop. Eden needed to solve the mystery.

"Where did the antique shop go?"

"What antique shop?" She continued to walk down the sidewalk and into the diner.

"Melissa, it couldn't have been a figment of both of our imaginations. We had the same experience, right?"

"Kind of, I guess. But I swear to you, Eden, you and that man were speaking French. Do you want to tell me what he said to you?"

"He knew that I was a Scorpio, which shocked me. That was the first thing that he said. Then he told me that if I was not prepared for what was about to transpire that I should quickly get into my vehicle and leave. It was a horrible warning that he gave me. I feel it was something way deeper. Almost like a dark omen. Melissa, the sole reason for him being there was to give me that warning. He said that my life would change forever if I didn't get my butt in the car and drive back to

Chicago. I was uneasy, but I made sure he didn't pick up on it. He said something about earth being a schoolhouse, and all lessons are not pleasant but necessary."

"How can you remember all that?"

"Melissa, I have a photographic memory. Besides, that is why I was so quiet yesterday. It's all I could think about. I couldn't even sleep last night. This is the strangest phenomenon that I've ever experienced. I'm a realist, and I expect everything to have a logical explanation. I don't know what to say. How would you explain it?"

"You're asking me? I don't even pretend to be a realist. Some things defy logic. Let's keep this our secret. We don't want Phyllis to think we're nut cases, but most of all, we want Nancy to keep her mind on the business at hand. What do you say?"

Melissa interpreted Eden's silence as consent. They walked away from the shop, neither woman turning for one final look.

NINETEEN

I don't know why you didn't go into town with Beth and Marcy. There isn't much to do here."

"You have been extremely nurturing to me with all I've been through concerning Bob. Who knows, maybe we can help heal each other." Nancy sat down on a large gray boulder and watched the waves gently caress the sandy shore. "I wish I could wave a magic wand and replace your pain with happiness."

"Ann, you're assuming that I am unhappy. I haven't said anything that would give you that idea."

"Let's be honest with each other, I can read the sadness in your face. I want to know what I can do to help."

"It's too late for me. Jerry has provided for me. He's been a good provider."

"Money is not a trophy for goodness or for success."

" At my age, what could I do? If I wanted to start over, I should have done it years ago."

"Age is just a state of mind. Can't you see your acres of diamonds? What if we helped you, all three of us? Phyllis, you have a wonderful career. You could find an attorney in Bear Junction and get back into being a legal secretary. You have energy and good health, at least physically."

"Jerry says that I couldn't make it in the real world. He says that I would not survive if it weren't for him. Unfortunately he's probably right." Phyllis sat down with Nancy and rubbed her hands together, as if to relieve the stress from her body "He is a very strict husband and father but he has always provided for us."

"It's funny that you're using all the words and excuses that I was so accustomed to using, especially the word 'provide'. Phyllis, because a man provides, doesn't give him the green light for abuse. Jerry is exactly like Bob, forever chiseling away at our self-esteem. Why would a husband and father need to be strict? Everything that has to do with family should be done out of love, not force. A marriage should be a partnership. I have never heard you use the word love, not one time. I would like to ask you something, and I promise that it won't go any further than here on this beach. He shows all the signs of being physically abusive, am I correct?"

"Yes, but only when I deserve it. Not very often, because I make a point of not upsetting him. I think that's what made our daughter become so rebellious. I have to admit, they had a strange relationship. In fact, she hasn't spoken to him in many years, and there doesn't seem to be anything I can do to patch things up. God knows, I've tried. Ann, he's not so bad when he's not drinking."

"Phyllis, do you think he was sexually abusive to your daughter?" The second the words were out of her mouth, she knew that she was far too abrupt.

Phyllis Anderson abruptly stood and faced Nancy.

"How can you even think such a thing? He would never in a million years do such a thing. How could you be so cruel? I might have been a coward in many ways but I have never been a moral coward. I am a good mother. You can't believe that I would ever have let anything like that happen to my daughter. Ann, I thought you and I were becoming friends."

It was obvious to Nancy that Phyllis was in denial. She took a deep breath and prayed that she could get through the walls Phyllis was building.

"Please sit down with me. I am your friend, and I'm just trying to understand. A simple yes or no would work. Phyllis, if it had never crossed your mind you would not be offended by my question. You would have merely answered my question. I watch Jerry. He needs to dominate everybody he comes in contact with. Beth is a strong woman, I could see how frustrated he was with her because trying to dominate her was fruitless. Jerry would be wise to steer clear of her. There's much more to Beth than he can even imagine. You are used to it, it's been part of your life so long that it seems normal and natural. I've noticed, you are doing precisely what I did with Bob, making excuses for his rude behavior. One short month ago, I was a totally different human being. Have you thought about anything that we spoke about yesterday?"

"Who are you three women? Why won't you give me a clue? You keep telling me what a good friend you are, but I don't even know your name or who you are. How can we be friends if I don't even have any base information about you? What's it like living in a big city like Chicago?"

"Phyllis, I will tell you everything in total and complete detail, if you'll just give me a little more time. You're starting to sound like Marcy, the way you're firing questions at me. I'll tell you this much, I am not from Chicago but I'll probably be moving there. Please, don't confide what I'm telling you in anybody else, especially Jerry. Promise me."

"Of course not. I don't see why it would matter. Who wouldn't you want me to confide in? The only person I talk to is Jerry." She hesitated. "Oh, I see. Why is it acceptable for me to tell you all my personal business, when you won't tell me nothing about yourself? I am beginning to doubt if you chose Wilderness Lodge by accident. There is more here than meets the eye."

"You have no reason to believe me, but what I say is the truth. In a short time, you'll know everything and it will all make perfect sense. Right now, why don't you just think of us as being your guardian angels? Everything that's concealed will come out in the open. You know, like the last piece of a puzzle."

Phyllis walked away, down the beach. Nancy gave her a head start and slowly followed. She squinted at the face of her watch as the reflection of the sun made it difficult to read.

"We should head back to the lodge."

"Why? It's not lunchtime, and I am sure the boat is not even close to being fixed yet. You want to escape from this serious conversation, and I can't say that I blame you. Sometimes looking at reality isn't pleasant, but necessary. Answer this for me. Do you think your daughter would become close with you if her father wasn't in the picture?"

"Maybe."

"Why? Answer the question honestly."

"He was a stern father. No child likes strong direction or to be reprimanded. Jerry was a little too hard on her. That's all. I used to pray a lot about it, but my prayers were never answered. I assumed that God had his reasons."

"God helps those who help themselves. Standing in traffic and praying that you won't get hit is an invitation to become road kill. I wish I could just grab you and wash all the pain from your soul, but I can't. Nobody could do that for me either even my friends. What I am saying is that I will offer you my hand to pull you out of that dark pit where you live but I can't force you to become well."

"Weren't you ever scared to leave him?"

"Of course, I spent every day of my life in fear. Remember, this is new to me, too. I'm still scared. I hate to think of what it's going to be like when we finally confront each other. My friends can help but they can't save me from that. It's the first step, which we have to do on our own. You must have had this in the back of your mind. You told me that you had some money put aside. How much? What do you fantasize about when you are alone? I'd wager that your fantasies are identical to the ones that I had. I wish you would tell me about them. No, I'll tell you about mine. I used to lie in bed thinking about running away with my stash of money. How I would change my identity. What kind of employment I would seek. I bought travel books by the dozen, dreaming of where I would take up residence. My family is gone and I don't have children so that left a clean slate. I didn't have many friends because Bob was so controlling that he hand selected all my friends. To be perfectly honest with you, I have no idea what I am going to do or where I'm going to live. There, now you know. You don't have to feel alone. You don't have to feel isolated, you're not alone. There you go, I spilled my guts and now it's your turn."

"Maybe I can't talk about it."

"Fine, okay. Let's go back to the paradise of Wilderness Lodge and forget we ever had this frigging conversation."

This time Nancy walked quickly and forceably toward the lodge. Phyllis sat, a desolately lone image with her head in her hands. Nancy continued to walk, intent on not looking back, even briefly. Nancy knew of the risk she took and, if she failed, the entire plan would be in jeopardy. She continued to briskly walk, hope against hope that all the poking and proding would not have been lost.

"Ann, wait."

Nancy stopped and turned. Phyllis was reluctantly walking toward her. Thank God, she thought. That was close.

"I'm just scared and need some time to think. It's too much, too soon. I'm not sure I'm strong enough or if I'll ever be strong enough."

"What would it take? I won't abandon you even when we leave this horrendous place. I need you to understand that this is an opportunity of a lifetime. Phyllis, this subject has been over talked. Let's leave it alone. I just briefly want to say one more thing, and then I promise that I'll shut up. By the time we leave, you will have experienced a life changing renaissance."

"What do you mean? I don't half understand what you are talking about."

"Enough, we agreed that we would not talk about it anymore."

Nancy could see Jerry Anderson in the distance still struggling with the large silver and red motor. She smiled as she saw him violently throw his hat down onto the pier. Eden was dead right, she sure knew how to cripple a motor.

Nancy heard him call out. "Phyllis get over here."

As Phyllis hurried to the old rough pier, she heard

her footsteps echo on the wood. Nancy stayed a safe distance but close enough to keenly observe. The wind had substantially picked up, and the black clouds that were so far in the distance were rapidly rolling in. Nancy hoped that Eden and Melissa would not get caught in a violent storm. She wondered if the lake was the component that made the weather so unpredictable. Remembering, when they came north on vacations, the bad storms were referred to as squalls. Thank God, Eden crippled the engine of the boat. Today would not be a good day for three inexperienced women to be sailing on Lake Superior. It was notorious for being the most violent of the Great Lakes. The gulls were predicting the storm with their loud mews. Where did they go when the wind and rain became overpoweringly fierce? They were smarter than some women, they had the good sense to remove themselves from the fury.

Nancy could hear Jerry's booming, frustrated voice. "Get the phone and call Jim Carver. Tell him to get his sorry ass out here to help me with this engine. We're going to have a hell of a storm."

Phyllis hurried into the side door of Wilderness Lodge, obliging her poor excuse of a husband. The air was thick and heavy, and the wind was becoming progressively wild. It pushed against Phyllis' body in an attempt to keep her standing stationary. The waves protested by foaming and hitting the shore with Herculean strength.

Nancy said softly to herself, "Eden and Melissa, where are you?"

TWENTY

Nancy found Phyllis as she was hanging up the phone's receiver. "Jerry's going to be fit to be tied." Her voice became shrill, as her eyes grew large. "I don't know what to tell him. Jim refuses to leave his house on a day like this. It's going to throw Jerry into a rage."

"Stop, stop it, Phyllis, just listen to yourself. You are just the messenger. You are passing on a message from Jim. He has the good sense not to come out in inclement weather to fix the engine of that damn boat. Nothing more, nothing less."

"Jerry is going to be so upset." She looked at Nancy as if trying to glean some approval, or at least some understanding. "It is just easier to try to keep him happy, don't you get it?"

"Yes, I understand far too well. Phyllis, I want you to march right down to that pier and relay the message, without apologies."

Nancy turned her back, not giving her any other opportunity to make excuses for that sorry excuse of a man. Nancy took the cell phone from her purse and dialed Eden. "I hope she has her phone turned on." She spoke mostly to herself.

Eden picked up after three rings. She didn't give

Nancy a chance to speak. "Yes, we are on our way back. Old Betty knows her stuff. She told us to drink up, our tea that is, and get our butts back here. Not in those exact words."

"Where are you right now?"

"About five minutes from the lodge. There are massive branches laying across the road, and the wind is doing its best to knock us into the ditch. This is not a good time to be talking on my cell, see you in a few minutes."

Nancy went to the back window and watched the black blanket of rain invade them from across the lake, assaulting like sheets in the wind. She took one step closer to the window that faced the pier. She watched Phyllis now standing with Jerry on the pier as they helped the two Milwaukee fishermen step out of their boat. Jerry reluctantly carried a large green and white cooler up the incline toward the lodge, grimacing under the weight.

The wind was so violent that every window in the lodge rattled. There was a deafening crack of thunder, and the lightning lit the lodge with an eerie glow.

The front door swung open, and Eden and Melissa stood in its threshold, soaked to the skin. Nancy ran to them, giving them both relieved hugs. "Where's Phyllis? Are we going to be able to talk for a few minutes?"

"She is down on the pier with Jerry, telling him something he doesn't want to hear. Hopefully, she won't be apologizing."

Melissa interrupted. "Well, how did things go today with her? Did you make any headway?"

"Swimmingly."

Melissa laughed and playfully poked her on her upper arm. "Have I ever told you that you're a dork?"

"Hourly. We need to talk fast. They'll be up her in a minute. It went so amazingly well that I believe tonight will be the night. Phyllis is ready to learn about Jerry's dirty little secret."

Eden shook her head in disbelief. "Wait a minute. How can you be sure?"

"Have a little confidence in her. She opened up and told me so many things, which included her dream about getting back in a legal secretary career. She has a lot of denial about Jerry's relationship with their daughter, though. That subject about ended our progress. I needed to back off. She said that her daughter needed a strict hand and no kid likes to be reprimanded. I know, more excuses. I am more convinced than ever that Jerry molested his own daughter."

Melissa's stomach tied into a knot. "How did you get her to open up?"

"I spilled all of my innards to her. Then she let loose, I'm sure she's ready. We need to get her alone tonight, away from Jerry and those fishermen."

The side door opened and Les, Gene, Jerry, and Phyllis stood dripping onto the rough wood lodge floor. Jerry was the first to speak. "That big maple tree is down, I've never seen wind like this. I'd like to know who's going to clean up that mess."

Gene smiled and kindly changed the subject. "You three are going to have a culinary delight tonight that you'll never forget. That is, if we can talk Phyllis into preparing the lake trout we caught. They are all cleaned and ready to go. We always clean the fish while we fish. It's too hard to do it later. I'll tell you something. Nobody can cook trout like Phyllis. If you don't mind, we want to change and rest for a little while before dinner." They both turned and made their way toward the door.

Nancy thought they seemed like nice guys but inspite of that brilliant observation, she hoped they would eat and run after dinner tonight.

Jerry broke the silence. "Get cooking, woman, don't just stand there."

Phyllis' voice carried crystal clear in the silent room. "You better dismount that barstool and get changed. You'll be pretty uncomfortable in the kitchen with wet clothes. Cooking fish is a big mess, and you will be helping me. Otherwise, they'll rot before I'll do all the work." Melissa's mouth visibly dropped open.

The only sound in that lodge was wind and rain, battering the old decrepit building. Nobody could bring herself to utter a word. Nancy's stomach grew a lump the size of a bowling ball. Only Nancy realized the enormity of the event that transpired in that ugly lodge. Nobody but Nancy could possibly understand the amount of strength it took for Phyllis to conjure up the courage to stand up to Jerry Anderson.

Nancy put her hand on Phyllis' shoulder. She smiled and spoke calmly as though nothing had happened. "Phyllis, do you have a can of pineapple in that kitchen?"

"Yes, I'm sure I do."

"Good, then you will all eat my outstanding pineapple upside down cake tonight. It's one of the few recipes that I've memorized. The truth is, it's the only recipe that I've memorized. By the time all of you come back in dry clothes you'll be greeted by the sweet aroma of my killer pineapple upside down cake." Nancy then proceded toward the swinging door that separated the lodge from the kitchen.

Jerry shouted aggressively. "I won't have my customers cooking."

Nancy hesitated and then turned. She flashed him a defiant smile and continued through the door of the kitchen.

"By the time we finish with this adventure, I'll be the weakest woman here." Eden put her hand under Melissa's elbow and guided her to the front door. "Let's hurry and change, we don't want to miss any more of the entertainment."

Melissa spoke with a coy lilt to her voice. "I hope Les is not a description of what lies beneath his zipper. Maybe I should find out."

"Some things never change."

Melissa and Eden ran through the cold black rain to their cabin. The wind blew the icy rain with such force that it felt like a million demons biting at Eden's face.

Melissa began to change her clothes. "This is stupid, we will be just as wet as before. Let's take dry clothes to the lodge and change there."

"I know what you're up to. You don't want to leave Nancy alone with Jerry. After dinner, let's tell Phyllis that we want to watch David Letterman with her. Hopefully, Jerry will be all tired out from his confrontation and his day playing Joe Mechanic with his boat engine."

"Eden, I am nervous. I think we should give it another day. I respect Nancy, but we have come too far to blow it now. Jerry Anderson is a bad habit that Phyllis has had for forty-five years. Habits are hard to break, especially in a few days. We need more time, I'm telling you."

"You might be right, have faith. Let's see how tonight goes, and we'll just play it by ear. I was impressed by the way Phyllis talked to him earlier. In fact, I couldn't believe it."

"I agree. But it could be the hype that Nancy laid on her earlier in the day. I know that my opinion doesn't mean much."

"Of course, it does, Melissa. Remember when we were kids? We called ourselves the three musketeers, all for one and one for all? Nothing's changed as far as I'm concerned. We're still the three musketeers."

"So far I haven't contributed much of anything to this project. You are definitely the brains. You're cool and calculating and seem to anticipate every bump and curve. Nancy has the warmth and sensitivity to be able to draw Phyllis to our side. She brings the human element. What do I bring? I'll tell you what I bring to this mix, nothing. A big fat round zero."

"Nothing? I'm cold and Nancy is warm. She and I

are the two extreme poles. I analyze it, and Nancy emotionalizes it. You, on the other hand, simplify everything. Melissa, you have the pure ability to look at a situation and tell it exactly like it is with no frills. It's a wonderful simple way of bringing us back to the reality of any situation. Don't put yourself down, you are positively the cornerstone of the foundation.

Nancy didn't lie, the fragrant spicy aroma of the pineapple cake permeated the lodge. They walked into the kitchen to find Jerry in one of his wretched moods. Phyllis was coating the fish as Nancy filled the dishwasher. Eden came dangerously close to laughing when she saw Jerry standing in the kitchen. He looked lost.

"How are my little house fraus' doing?" Melissa elbowed her and forced a smile.

Jerry narrowed his eyes and gave her a lethal stare. He washed his hands with the green liquid soap that sat on the edge of the sink and slowly dried them on the wet kitchen towel. Without comment, he left the kitchen. Les and Gene had not yet arrived for their anticipated feast. Jerry decided to pour himself a double scotch and water while he waited for them. The scotch, the barstool, and the empty bar area felt comfortable and familiar to him.

He mumbled aloud, audible to nobody but himself. "House fraus, is it? Eden McNeal, you arrogant, self obsessed little bitch. We'll see how cocky you are when old Jerry brings you and your friends down. It makes my mouth water just thinking about it."

Melissa loved the warmth, smells and comfort that

the time in the kitchen brought. She decided that Nancy was right. Phyllis Anderson was a naturally kind person. This wild fiasco would be so much easier if she was as evil as her husband. Melissa wondered how Phyllis could possibly have hooked up with such a bastard. If the plan works, she thought, what are they going to do with Phyllis? Take her back to Chicago or Rockton? Melissa was beginning to have doubts that the plan could possibly work. Right or wrong, nobody can control the feelings anybody has for anybody else. How far are we going to go to split up Phyllis and Jerry Anderson?"

Melissa took the plates and silverware and began to set the table. Jerry walked across the room with the intent to harass her. He stood there looking at the table. He made a point of straightening one of the table services that Melissa put down.

Jerry grimaced, as he inadvertadly put his hand on his stomach. "That frigging boat tied my guts in knots. Too bad one of you girls isn't a doctor. I could use some stomach meds right now."

The edges of Melissa's lips turned up as she looked at him. "I am a doctor. Please allow me to give you some free medical advice. You could fart or have some more of that whiskey, that'll cure it." She thought for a moment, with confusion on her face. "Why do you assume that one of us isn't a doctor?"

He rubbed the back of his neck, to give the impression that he didn't care. "Sweetie, I don't assume anything. I know. Let me warn you now, don't ever make the mistake of underestimating me. Besides, it's pretty obvious that you probably didn't even make it through high school. Who knows, maybe not even grade school."

"It's amazing that I did, considering the low quality of some of the teachers I had in grade school."

"Somehow, I think that whatever you got, you deserved." The look he flashed at Melissa gave her the uncanny feeling that he knew something. But how could he?

TWENTY-ONE

Melissa had the good sense to know that to stab him in the gut with a table knife would be inappropriate. Being her hidden fantasy for so many years, the temptation nearly overwhelmed her. What justice, she thought, if I killed him with a knife. The weapon he used to threaten her into submission. If he touches me, even for a second, she thought, I'd have to sink this knife into his heart. She took a deep breath and counted to ten to regain her composure. She started to become light headed. When Jerry reached in front of her to pick up the silverware, Melissa had flashbacks of what he did to her so many years ago. He picked up a table knife, smiled, and ran his thumb over the tip of it seductively. Just the sight of what he had just done had her stomach flipping. She had to run, flee or her brain would shatter into a million crazy pieces. That stale scent of his body and him standing with the knife brought memories that flooded back from the dark recesses of her mind. Their eyes locked, dark with anger, unsaid words resonated between them.

The door violently flew open, crashing against the wall. "Sorry", Les made a funny face and offered a red-faced apology. "This wind is a bitch. But, in spite of the wind, I could still smell the fish cooking a hundred yards away."

Gene, apparently a bit more introverted, waited to speak. "Any weather report for tomorrow? I hope we'll be able to get out on the lake."

"You're welcome to watch the news tonight. It'll be interesting to find out how much damage has been done, even though it's not over yet." Jerry took another sip of his scotch.

Phyllis came out of the kitchen triumphantly, as she carried a large platter of lake trout propped on one hand high in the air. Les and Gene whistled and cheered. She smiled and took a quick bow.

Melissa put her hand on Les' shoulder. "It was generous of you and Gene to share your catch with us."

"Who else could cook them like Phyllis?" He pulled out the chair next to him and motioned for Melissa to sit down. Melissa noticed that he used a liberal dose of aftershave.

Even Eden, with her discriminating taste, thought the evening meal was extraordinary. The negative was Jerry Anderson who sat across the table from her, constantly felt his eyes on her as though he was peeling off the layers of an onion. This persisted much of the meal. Eden sensed something was wrong, but she couldn't quite put her finger on it. She looked at Melissa with puzzlement on her face. When she turned back, Jerry's eyes were still fixed on her. She still remembered that sinister look. It was the same look he had so many years ago when he lured her to his house after school. The same look when he forced her to take off her clothes, and he stood studying her tiny naked body. God, she thought, how I hate him. Maybe just taking Phyllis away is not enough. Killing him would be so sweet.

The meal seemed to last for an extremely long time. Finally, Jerry invited Les and Gene to join him for a drink at the bar while the women cleaned up the kitchen. Melissa pulled Eden aside while Nancy was in the dining room collecting dirty dishes. "I think he knows something. I'm sure of it."

"I got that same feeling. But I don't know how it's possible." Nancy approached with a stack of plates. "Come here we need to talk. Melissa and I both think there is something going on with Jerry. We think he knows something. Are we paranoid?"

"He said something to me earlier. It wasn't what he said, but the spirit in which he said it. I don't think all of us would be having the same feelings if there were nothing there. We should keep in mind that forgiving him doesn't make him right, but it makes us free. Hate is the cancer of the soul." Even Nancy was surprised at her own words.

Melissa took the heavy plates from Nancy and set them on the rickety reception desk. "No, sweetie, don't even go down that road. We are not here for forgiveness. If it was forgiveness that we were after, we could have just written him a nice warm fuzzy letter. That forgiveness thing might have worked for you, but it sure the hell won't work for me. Look, if you are having a problem with our plan, it's time we knew."

"No, Melissa, no problem. We are still standing strong together, the three musketeers, remember? It's just hard to break old habits. What I said was something I used to tell myself, all these years, to help keep my sanity. It seemed to help, both with Jerry Anderson and Bob."

"What do you think Jerry knows? Do you think he figured out our identities? We've been so careful."

Melissa threw up her hands in surrender. "Who the hell cares what he knows? He'll soon find out anyway. It would be a lot better, though, if we could do it on our own terms and in our own time. Should we step things up and tell Phyllis now? Our time might be running out."

Eden was stern. "We won't panic. That would be self-defeating and put Jerry Anderson in charge. Remember, we're still holding all the cards. This is just a hiccup in our plan. Melissa is absolutely right. Who cares what he knows? Ask yourself if it really makes any difference if he knows everything. How will that change a thing? We need to stay focused." Eden felt a twinge of guilt over her secret. Jerry looked across the room at the threesome and gave them a sly smile. "He could be bluffing. His ego was hurt when he found that note in the luggage. He could be just trying to annoy us. You know, pretending he knows more than he actually does."

"I wonder how long Les and Gene plan on hanging

around? We can't do anything until they leave. Gene was complaining at dinner that he was about ready to fall asleep. That afternoon on the lake, trying to battle the storm had to be exhausting." Nancy picked up her plates. "I better get back in there. This can't look like a meeting."

"Are you going to watch Letterman with me tonight?" Phyllis had her back to Nancy as she was loading the dishwasher. "Jerry goes to bed early. We can have a girls' night, open a bottle of wine, and watch Letterman. Gene and Les said that they were going to turn in early."

As they walked toward the bar, Gene and Les were already saying good night to Jerry. They bid their goodnights to everyone and left the lodge.

"Good." Melissa whispered to Eden. "Two down and one to go."

"Jerry looks pretty comfortable. What do you make of that? He's usually in bed by now." Eden leaned closer as they approached him. "I say he has something up his sleeve. I wish that we could identify it."

Jerry went behind the bar. "What would you ladies like to drink?"

"Red wine for all of us would be fine." Nancy was fidgeting. You had a hectic day, I would think that with all the time you spent working on that motor you would be worn out. Don't feel like you have to entertain us, we are just going to watch the news and Letterman then go back to our cabin."

"Trying to get rid of me? I am not at all tired. I feel like I haven't really had a chance to get to know you lovely ladies."

Eden wished that Nancy hadn't committed to the news and Letterman. She didn't think she could stand two hours with that ass hole.

Half way through the news, the door of the lodge burst open, and Bob Benson stormed in. "Surprise."

Jerry laughed harder than they ever heard him. "So you think you were pulling one over on me, did you? Never make the mistake of playing me for the fool. I had your license plates traced and, low and behold, it was Nancy and Bob Benson from Rockton."

Nancy sat paralyzed on her barstool barely breathing. Eden jumped up as she put her hand into her purse. She felt the comforting coolness of the revolver.

"You look like a fucking whore with that hideous bleached blonde hair. Get into that Explorer and be prepared to drive." His face scarlet red, Bob looked as though he was courting a heart attack. "What are you doing up here with Jerry Anderson? He said you all gave him phony names. Are you sleeping with him?"

"You idiot. How dare you speak to me like that? Sleeping with him would be about as enjoyable as smashing my finger with a hammer. Bob, the days of you telling me what to do are long past."

"That's my Explorer, and I'm telling you to haul your ass back to Rockton tonight."

"As usual, it's all about things, isn't it? Well your things will soon shrink to 50%. I'm going to divorce you, Bob. By the way, don't you remember? That Explorer is in my name for some tax loop hole."

Bob, furious, stepped toward Nancy fully intent on hitting her. Eden deftly stepped between them. "I wouldn't, Melissa just dialed 911. The police will be here soon. And if they're not, four strong women can easily take care of you."

"Step aside. This is between a man and his wife. Something you wouldn't know anything about "

"I'll step aside if Nancy tells me to. It seems to me that she needs her friends a hell of a lot more than she needs you."

"I said to get your ass in that Explorer, now. We need to leave this freak show."

"The only two freaks in this freak show are you and Jerry Anderson." The shock of everyone in the room was colossal. "Bob, the police are on their way. Either leave on your own volition, or you will be forced to leave. I really mean leave, not lurk around, thinking that you can still bully me tomorrow. If you don't get out of here now, I'll be forced to file a restraining order on you. And don't think, even for a minute that I won't."

Jerry spoke up. "I rented Bob a cabin for the night. We knew he'd be arriving late and...."

Phyllis interrupted "Of course, if it had to do with evil, I should have known that you would have had your fingers in it. It just killed you, didn't it? It made you crazy that I was enjoying myself with Beth, Ann and Marcy. You couldn't stand to see me experience a little joy in my life."

"What a joke. They didn't even think enough of you to tell you their real names. For your information, Phyllis, it's Eden, Nancy and Melissa. They made a fool out of you just like they tried to make fools out of Bob and me."

"Jerry, you have no idea what you're talking about. Don't make me choose what team I'm going to play for. You'll regret my choice. It sounds to me like you and Bob would have a lot in common. It wouldn't break my heart if you left together."

"What's come over you? What kind of craziness have these bitches put in your head?"

Bob glared at Eden. "You have no idea what these women are capable of. Look what Eden and Melissa did to my wife. We had a great relationship until they got into the mix. They hate men and try to ruin every decent marriage they can get their claws into."

He quickly stepped forward and grabbed Nancy by the arm in an attempt to drag her to the door. Nancy abruptly yanked her arm free.

"You will never touch me again. Do you understand?"

Eden was relieved that she didn't have to bring out her gun even though she was prepared. She wanted that to be her ace in the hole, to be used only in the case of dire emergency.

"Bob, the police are on their way. Display some vague hint of intelligence and get out of here, fast. Nancy no longer feels that there is anything worth saving, and you would be wise to put the blame where it belongs. That would be with yourself."

"You fucking bitch, I...."

The door opened and in walked Sheriff Cromwell before Bob could finish his sentence. "Who phoned 911?"

Melissa took a calming breath. "I did. I am Melissa Perkins. I phoned because Bob Benson was becoming loud and violent. I was frightened for Nancy's safety."

Jerry laughed. "Sorry, Sheriff, we didn't mean to waste your time. This gentleman has just come here to pick up his wife and take her home where she belongs. There's no problem."

"Which one of you women is his wife? This better not be a false alarm."

Sheriff Cromwell was a box shaped man of about forty. Everything about him was square, including his flat top hair cut, right out of the sixties. He looked like he would be the kind of man a person would want on his side, not as an enemy. "This is a bad night to get me out here. I hope for your sake it's not a false alarm. I don't look kindly on that. There have been a lot of calls today because of the weather. This better not have been a waste of my valuable time."

"Officer, I drove here from Rockton, Illinois, to take

my wife home. I don't mean to make anyone's life miserable. She and I are going to drive back tonight. Isn't that right, Honey?"

Bob replaced his look of rage to a look of patience and calm. He stepped toward Nancy to put his arm around her.

Nancy stepped back. "I warn you, don't touch me. Sheriff Cromwell, I came here with my two friends to escape this man. He's abusive with me, both mentally and physically. I'm here to get my thoughts together and make plans for my future. He has been dogging me constantly, and I am sick of his threats. I lied to Jerry Anderson about my real name. Some how he found out and phoned Bob without my permission or knowledge. I planned to leave here soon, in a day or two. I fully intend to get a divorce. I'm afraid of this man and I want him to leave me alone. I can tell that he plans on hurting me. Do I need to get a restraining order against him or can you figure out how to get through to him?"

"Can I figure out a way to get through to him? Depends on Mr. Benson. Why don't you tell me, Mr. Benson? Are you going to go back to Rockton, Illinois, or are you going to go to jail? It's your call."

Jerry walked over to the sheriff and put his hand on his shoulder. "Come on Sheriff, it's not at all like it seems. We fellows have to stick together."

"Back off, Jerry. You have enough sense to know that you broke the law by making that phone call to Mr.

Benson. You better hope that Nancy Benson doesn't pursue it. This has become a criminal matter. I don't think it's anything you want to become involved with."

"Bob Benson will be spending the night in one of our cabins."

"No, he won't. He will either be on his way back to Rockton or he will have accommodations in the Bear Junction jail. What's it going to be, Mr. Benson?"

"Sheriff, it's late. Can't I at least spend the night in town?"

"Okay, but I'm giving you fair warning. If I get another call, you will be staying in my hotel, the Bear Junction jail. I want you to leave Nancy Benson alone. And before I escort you out of here, I have something to say to you, Jerry. Don't get involved in anybody else's marital issues or you'll end up in court."

The sheriff walked Bob to his car. "I'm going to follow you to town. Right before we get to Bear Junction there is a small motel. That's where I want you to stop. That place always has openings. I'll walk in with you, and you'll give Craig your car keys to keep safe for you until you leave in the morning."

"I'm not giving anybody my car keys."

"Well then, if you are in the mood to drive, you can head back to Rockton tonight. Like I said before, the choice is yours. Craig will phone me in the morning when you are ready to leave. Then I'll call your wife to warn her that you're mobile. It's just to keep you honest.

Somehow, I get the impression that you're a hot head. I can just picture you heading back to make some more trouble at Wilderness Lodge. Hey, if I let you stay in town, you better promise not to be cranky." His laugh was deep and guttural. "Don't get any brilliant ideas. Bear Junction doesn't have a taxi service. And just for your own personal information, Craig is my brother."

TWENTY-TWO

Jerry returned to his customary place behind the bar and poured himself another scotch. He drank it all in one long gulp and promptly poured himself another. This time not drinking the amber liquid with such haste.

The color had drained from Nancy's face, making her appear pasty and gaunt. "Nancy, would you like a drink before we go back to our cabin? It might help to relax you." Eden was generally concerned about her.

"No. No thank you. I'm fine. Are we going to stay and watch Letterman?"

"None of us are in the mood for Letterman tonight." Eden wrote her cell phone number on the back of a paper beer napkin and handed it to Phyllis. "My cell phone will be on all night. I promise not to turn it off. Jerry is pretty angry with you right now, plus he's well on the way to getting drunk. Call us and we will be here for you in a heartbeat. I noticed that there's a roll away bed in our cabin. Feel free to use it if you want to."

"Thank you for everything. Don't worry about me. If Jerry goes into one of his tirades, I can handle it. After all, I'm used to him. Please, just take care of Nancy. She's my hero. This was a horrible ordeal for her." Phyllis turned and slyly slid the napkin into her pocket.

The walk back to the cabin was bone chilling cold. The temperature had dropped considerably. The wind wasn't quite as fierce, but shook the trees with angry groans. The drizzle was unrelenting as the women made their way to the cabin. The miniature wood porch on the front of their cabin creaked under the weight of the three women. Nobody noticed or cared that the cabin was exceptionally clammy and cold. It was the events of the evening consuming on their thoughts. Nancy was in better humor after a hot shower and clean pajamas.

"Eden, it's your turn to make coffee in the morning."

"I always have to do everything." Eden artificially whined. "Nancy, how does it feel to be psychologically single?"

"Relieved, free, and scared."

Melissa resumed her role as mother hen. "Scared, what do you mean scared? Being single isn't half bad. Tell me, are you afraid he'll be back here tonight or in the morning? I don't think he has the balls. That sheriff put the fear of God in him. Bob Benson wouldn't want to sully his sterling reputation by going to the Bear Junction jail."

"Melissa, I realize that you know Bob better than Eden, but nobody's going to tell Bob what to do. And that includes Sheriff Cromwell. Don't doubt that Bob will be back. We still have another day and night to accomplish our mission. I don't know about you, but I have no intention of letting Bob screw it up. I've come to terms with him, and I refuse to allow him to intimidate me. You don't have to remind me that I passed the point of no return. I know that there will be no going back to my old life in Rockton."

Melissa put her arm around Nancy's shoulders. "How do you feel about that?"

"I feel like a little girl off to her first day at school. It's like the whole world is opening up for me, and there are no longer any restrictions. Although it's a little scary with nobody to protect me."

"What are you talking about? You have two good friends to protect you. Actually three good friends, we can't forget about Phyllis. I developed an all new respect for her tonight. She's a gutsy lady. I've got to say that I believe you're right, Nancy. Phyllis is ready."

Melissa tried to talk and brush her teeth at the same time. "I hate this place. I hate Jerry. I hate this moldy room. I hate the bugs. I hate the suspense. I sure the hell didn't want to prolong it another day, but thanks to Bob we'll be stuck here indefinitely."

Eden interrupted. "Could you repeat that one more time, I'm not retarded yet. Here's the plan. We'll hang out all day. Then tomorrow night, after Jerry goes to bed, we'll make our move. It will be time to tell Phyllis about her esteemed hubby. Oh, my God, I just thought of something." Eden hesitated before she continued to speak. "He knows who we are. Of course, he has to remember molesting each and every one of us. As much as the booze has eaten away at his brain, I'm sure he hasn't forgotten one sick detail. Because of Bob our cover's been blown. He has to be suspicious of our motives. We told him that we were here to help Nancy escape from Bob. Well, now what's keeping us? Do you think he knows what we're up to?"

"Jerry isn't stupid. He's evil, but not stupid. We can bet that he has cooked up a scheme." Nancy frowned. "This has gotten way out of hand. What are we going to do?"

Eden got off the side of her bed and faced both of her friends. "Nothing, other than continue on with our plan of action. What can he do other than ask us to leave? If he does, then he'll risk us spilling the beans to Phyllis. He's devious and we'd be fools to trust him. But as far as I'm concerned, it's business as usual. It's going to be really difficult to hang around here all day tomorrow, but I don't think we should go into town. We need to concentrate on Phyllis, she might not be quite ready. Nancy, please spend some more time with her. Besides, Jerry must feel extremely threatened right now, and I'm kind of worried about her safety. Let's suggest to Phyllis that we want a late dinner tomorrow, and we'll watch Letterman with her. It would be too suspicious to spend the whole day drinking and eating in the lodge. So grab your books and towels, and we'll spend the day on that nasty rocky beach."

Nancy became solemn. "I think we should all pray tonight. Whatever happens will take place tomorrow. It will be the culmination of all our efforts."

"Whatever works for you, honey."

"Melissa, when you pray you make a demand on

what already belongs to you. It seems to me that God is somebody you would want on our side."

"I've tried prayer and it seems like God turned a deaf ear."

"Sometimes we don't even recognize the answers to our prayers because they're not answered the way we prayed them. I'd rather pray big and get half of what I pray for than to pray for nothing and get all that I pray for. Melissa, knock and keep knocking. Don't be stubborn about asking God for help."

"You pray, and I'll grieve. I'll grieve over our wasted childhood. Nancy, this subject definitely needs to be changed. On the bright side, we don't have to use those stupid fake names anymore." Melissa took a napkin out of her purse. "I've still got the number for those two people we met at the bar. Remember Tammy and Bob?"

"What are you thinking? It's complicated enough without dragging in anybody else." Nancy playfully threw a sock at her. "I think Sheriff Cromwell is our new best friend. Didn't you get the idea that Jerry wasn't one of his favorite people? Or Bob either, for that matter? Bear Junction isn't that big. He knows where Bob is staying. I wouldn't doubt if he phones Bob in the morning, and they combine forces. That would be our worst nightmare." Melissa turned off the light, removed her slippers, and climbed into her cold lumpy bed. "On second thought, it might be a blessing in disguise. It would give us a great opportunity to call Sheriff

Cromwell and have the bastard arrested. Everything would be worthwhile just for that split second of seeing Bob dragged off in handcuffs. After all, he's been warned about bothering Nancy again Maybe we better stick close together tomorrow. Let's take a vote about leaving? This is going to be the last chance."

"No." "No." "No." Those were the last three words spoken in that dingy cabin that night.

TWENTY-THREE

Even though they unilaterally decided not to set the alarm and vowed to sleep late, old habits die hard. Eden was the first to use the bathroom. Melissa heard the water and the pipes banging through the thin walls. She squinted her eyes to be able to see the small face on the travel clock. It reflected eight thirty. She said quietly, but still audibly. "Brace yourself, today is the day." She didn't realize that Nancy was already awake until she spoke.

"You're right, today is the day. I could hardly sleep last night. My nerves are completely frazzled. I laid awake and kept going back to dark side of my memories. I will never understand how Jerry Anderson could have derived any pleasure out of hurting three innocent little girls. And how could we, all three of us, kept mute all these years? We are all intelligent people."

Eden finished her shower and spoke from the bathroom. "Nancy, it took so long because shame and guilt are very close relatives. He conditioned us to believe that what he was doing to us was normal, and worst of all, that we wanted it. I feel such rage when I think about that monster. Are we ever going to be okay? I try not think how different our lives would be if just one of us would have told."

"Would it really have been that different? The damage was already done. It was done at the moment of his first touch."

"We don't know how many other little girls he molested before or after us. If he was in prison, he might have felt the ravage of rape. That would have been justice in the true base form." Eden still had not left the bathroom. She spoke from the partially opened door. "He poisoned our lives and today we'll take the antidote to rid ourselves of his poison."

"Whenever I feel insecure, all I have to do is listen to you, Eden. You've always got the right words, and you're so determined."

"Hey, I've also got the gun." Eden emerged from the confines of the bathroom.

Melissa and Nancy took one look at her and broke into hysterical laughter. It was nearly impossible for Melissa to regain enough composure to talk. "How many rolls of toilet paper did that take?"

Eden stood in the middle of their bedroom in her swimsuit. It was a conservative green print two-piece. She stuffed the bodice with washcloths to make her look like she was a 42E cup. Her size two body looked like it was going to fall forward onto the floor on her face. Eden didn't crack a smile and looked puzzled at their laughter. "I've always been extremely well endowed. I am surprised that neither of you ever noticed. Do I sense a little jealousy here?" Eden reached into the swimsuit and retracted the hand towels. She threw them on top of her bed. "I am going to spend some quiet time down on the beach. I need a cold swim before breakfast and I've got some thinking to do. I'll meet you two at the lodge in about an hour."

A look of concern passed over Nancy's face. "I thought we had an agreement. Didn't we agree to stay close today? It's too risky separating, especially now that Jerry knows who we are."

"Don't worry about me. I've got the gun."

"Exactly, which would mean that we don't." Nancy was adamant.

"One hour, that's all. Then I promise that we'll stick together like glue." Eden grabbed a towel before she turned the door handle. She proceeded to walk onto the old wooden porch. "Oh my God." All color had drained from her face as she ran back inside and shut the door in panic. "What the hell are we going to do now? Call somebody, quick."

"Who is out there?" Melissa screamed as she ran to the window and peeked through the slit in the drapes. "There's a big bear on our front porch. I thought it was Jerry or Bob. I'd rather a bear."

"If we call down to the lodge, Phyllis will send Jerry. He's sleeping right now. Do we want to waste the few hours of private time with Phyllis by waking him up? Just sit down and don't call. We need to think about this problem. There's no food out there so I'm sure he won't want to hang out very long." As Nancy pulled back the drapes, the bear stared back at her through the window. "So Eden do you still want to go down to the lake for your refreshing morning swim?"

"Maybe not." She said meekly.

Melissa sat for a moment contemplating their dilemma. "I've got an idea. We have those apples that we bought in town. Let's throw some and when the bear goes to retrieve them, we'll make a mad dash for the lodge."

"Are you going to be the thrower or the runner?" By now Eden was sitting on the side of her bed.

"Hell no. I'm just the planner, not the thrower or the runner. To be honest, I'd be afraid to leave here even if the bear decided to go home. Anyway, how long does it take a big bear to eat a little apple? Eden, you're the brains of the outfit. What are we going to do?"

"How would I know? Let's call Jerry, coat him with honey and let the bear eat him."

"Seriously, we can't spend the day here because of that bear. Think of something. Let's call the lodge and talk to Phyllis."

"No, absolutely not. She'll wake Jerry and we'll be stuck with him all day. Today is the big thrust. We need to spend as much private time with Phyllis as possible." Eden walked back to the window. "See, he's gone. We must have bored him."

Nancy let out an unsteady breath. "I'm still afraid to leave. What if he's waiting for us? They don't call this place Bear Junction for nothing." Without discussion, she took her phone out of her purse and dialed the lodge. "Hello, Phyllis. Yes. Listen, we have a slight problem. No. Don't wake up Jerry. We need your advice. A big bear was hanging out on the front porch. What? Jake? You name the bears? I don't know about that. He didn't look harmless when he was looking in the window. I don't know. Maybe a friendly dog or cat, but.... Yea, but.... okay I'll tell Eden and Melissa. Would you please?"

"Phyllis said that Jake the bear is like a pet."

Eden threw up her hands. "Victor is wild and weird enough for my taste. I'm not making Jake my new best friend. No negotiating, that's just the way it is."

"Phyllis is on her way up here as we speak. She said that she would walk us down to the lodge. Eden, you might want to put some clothes on."

"Let's have breakfast and either suggest to Phyllis that we all go swimming or go into Bear Junction to shop. We need to think about separating her from Jerry today. Especially if we plan to tell her the big secret tonight."

When Melissa went into the bathroom, Nancy lowered her voice. "Eden, today is Melissa's birthday. She has no idea that I remembered. Let's surprise her."

It was an enormous relief when Phyllis knocked softly at their door, even though they had to draw their conversation to an end. "Come on my little chickens and let mommy hen protect you from the big bad bear."

They laughed. "Phyllis, today is Melissa's birthday. She doesn't know that we remembered. Any ideas?"

"Do you want to include me?"

"Of course, we do. Let's keep the birthday a secret and surprise her. Do you have any ideas?"

"There's a small town about thirty miles from here, Cranston. It has great gift shops and boutiques. In fact, not much else other than one trendy little café. I'm not even sure if it is still open. They have really strange hours. We can treat her to lunch and if she sees something in one of the shops, we can sneak back and buy it."

Melissa came out of the bathroom dressed and ready to leave. Phyllis stood with her mouth open. "You have curly red hair."

"Thank God, I don't have to wear that damn wig anymore. I had a nightmare that my hair fell out and I had to wear that dowdy brown wig for the rest of my life."

"I can't imagine why you girls cooked up that elaborate plan just to hide from Bob Benson. He's such a mousy guy."

"Well, you got a taste of the true Bob last night. Mousy wouldn't be one of my descriptive words, at least in private. His true colors come out when we're alone. He's cruel and aggressive when nobody else is around. Phyllis, we decided to stay close together today. I don't trust Bob. There is no way he's going to get back in his car and drive back to Rockton without causing me some major trouble." The gravel of the driveway crunched under their feet as they made their way to the lodge. "If we decide to go swimming today, will Jake be joining us?"

"No. He has his own fishing hole. Besides, his swimsuit is at the cleaners. If you decide to go swimming, let me know. I'll go down with you. Les and Gene are already out on the lake fishing and said they weren't going to be eating dinner with us tonight. They are going to eat in town. So, if you need my services, let me know. I don't have too much to do today. Besides, I've decided not to be at Jerry's beck and call anymore. There's one thing for sure, he's not too happy about the change that's come over me since you showed up. But, I will have hell to pay after you leave."

"Phyllis, we're tentatively planning to leave tomorrow, so let's make the most of today. We can go swimming and shopping in Cranston, then eat a big fancy expensive lunch, my treat." All the while Eden was talking, her eyes were darting first to the right and then to the left. "Sorry, my concentration level is not at its peak when I am scouting for vicious animals."

"Am I to assume that we're not going to be inviting Jake?"

"You're really having a good time with this Jake thing, aren't you Phyllis?

Melissa got a stone in her shoe and asked everybody to halt while she removed it. "This is, without a doubt, the best part of the trip. Eden out of control. It's great to have a black bear in charge."

"Shut up, Melissa."

"I have a special breakfast prepared, so let's hurry before it gets burned or cold."

"This place smells like heaven. Not that I would ever know. What is that aroma?" Eden was sniffing the air. "The smell is so interesting. In fact, it smells familiar."

"It is something that men don't seem to appreciate. At least the men who come here to fish or hunt. What you are smelling is curried eggs."

Eden volunteered. "My mother always makes curried eggs for Christmas breakfast. It's kind of a tradition. I'm not sure if it's the tradition that makes them special or if it's the actual flavor. Curried eggs are probably an acquired taste. I see it as an omen that today is going to be a special day."

"Well, it sure the hell isn't Christmas, Eden. It's going to be hot and humid today. I am so glad I don't have to wear that suffocating wig anymore." She ran her fingers through her bright red curls. "They could use that thing to get secrets out of war criminals. I'm going to send it to the Pentagon so they can use it on Sadam."

"Sadam in that wig. There are some visuals that I don't want to have imprinted on my brain." Eden was already setting the table. "So what you're saying is that you're free today to spend some time with us tourists?"

"The whole day. I'm going to do something that I've never done before. I'm going to write Jerry a note and then leave. In fact, I'm going to do one better. I'm going to tell him to make his own lunch and I'll be back when

I get here. He doesn't even let me to go grocery shopping without his blessing."

"Blessing? Hmm, strange choice of words."

TWENTY-FOUR

"Swimming or shopping, what will we do first?" Nancy recognized the shakiness in Phyllis' voice. "It's getting late and Jerry might show up soon to give me a hassle about leaving. I say I'll write my note and get out of this place as fast as I can. Should I pack us a picnic lunch?"

"No way, after that wonderful breakfast you deserve to be pampered. Besides, Eden offered to buy us all lunch. And we're going to order the most expensive things on the menu. We won't let you get her off the hook. She has a magical charge card that knows no limit."

"Melissa, you're so lucky that we love you because you're enormously obnoxious."

Out of the corner of her eye, Nancy spied Jerry lumbering up the incline to the lodge. Spare tire hanging over his baggy pants, it was easy to see that his breath was labored. He was wearing a long sleeved plaid shirt and an old fishing hat. Even from a distance it was noticeable, the lines on his face from years of drink and smoke. She opted to say nothing as the gravel crunched under the Explorer's tires. They slowly left the lodge parking lot. Nancy thought that some things were better left unsaid. Melissa was driving and Nancy sat in the back with Phyllis. She thought that Phyllis was particularly talkative and happy. It could be the weather, which was warm and sunny, but somehow Nancy thought it went deeper.

"If we're going to Cranston, you better turn right at the next road. Go straight if you need anything in Bear Junction."

Melissa continued to drive past the exiting road. "I need to buy some hair stuff now that I don't have to wear that gnarly wig. You can sit tight while I run into the drugstore. It will only take me few minutes. Does anybody else need anything?"

Nancy cracked open the window when they stopped in front of the Bear Junction Drug Store. "I want to go in with you. I need something for my stomach. It's been doing flip flops ever since we left Oak Park."

There was a front and a back door to the old brick drug store. Obviously, it hadn't been updated in about forty years. The doors weren't modernized or expanded to accommodate the automatic sliding doors.

"Bear Junction makes Rockton look like it's out of the Jetsons."

There wasn't any rhyme nor reason to the layout of the drugstore, so it took some substantial time for Nancy to find the aisle with the stomach remedies. She finally spotted them toward the back of the store. To save time, Melissa and Nancy split up. As Nancy approached the door that went to the back parking lot, she felt a firm hand around her upper arm. Bob was physically pulling her out of the store. It happened so fast that she didn't have an opportunity to call for help. When they got outside, she glared up into his face. The bright red rage went clear up to his hairline, with the vein on his forehead pulsating.

"You get in the car now or I'll beat the shit out of you right here in the parking lot."

"I'm not going anywhere with you Bob, so you better get on with it and start beating me. It won't be the first time, will it? But I will promise you it will be the last." She had a flashback of the agreement that Melissa, Eden and she made, not to split up even for a minute. "How did you know that we were going to the drug store?" Bob still had a painful grip on her upper arm.

The only time she ever looked attractive was when she was scared, he thought. "Don't play me for the fool. I saw the Explorer whiz by my motel and then I waited a few minutes for my chance. Get your ass in my car before I have to get mad. And you won't like it when I get mad."

Melissa walked to the counter with her three hair items. The elderly lady at the register looked uncomfortable, bored and unfriendly.

"I seem to have lost track of my friend. She planned on buying some stomach antacid. Blonde? This isn't a very big store and I've looked down every isle. Did you see her leave? She's probably waiting for me in the car."

"She didn't end up buying anything. She left with some man out the back door."

"Call 911 and get the sheriff over here. Quickly I'll get my friends. Please hurry this is an emergency. Tell him that Bob Benson has my friend Nancy." She look at the phone as though it was some kind of a foreign object.

Melissa, knowing it was a lost cause, roughly grabbed the phone out of her hand and dialed 911. "This is Melissa Perkins. Please get Sheriff Cromwell to the back parking lot of the *Bear Junction Drug Store* immediately. Bob Benson has taken Nancy against her will."

Melissa left her purchases on the counter and ran out the front door. The windows of the Explorer were open.

"Bob took Nancy. Hopefully they're still in the back parking lot. We've called the sheriff."

Melissa jumped into the drivers seat and nearly hit the car in front of her. She drove quickly to the back entrance of the store, at one point going over the curb. As Melissa drove into the back parking lot, she noticed that Bob and Nancy were the only people there. They faced each other and spoke loudly. Bob raised his hand and slapped Nancy across the face with such force that she fell onto the gravel of the parking lot. Melissa stopped the Explorer so quickly that the engine died.

The only words spoken were from Melissa. "That ass hole."

In unison, all three women jumped out of the Explorer, leaving the doors gaping open. "You better tell those bitches to back off or you'll get hurt."

Eden who had remained silent until now said, "Let's get him."

Eden flew at him like a wild cat. She had taken a self-defense class over a year ago and didn't forget one minute detail of anything that she learned. She poked his eyes and when he took his hands off Nancy, she used it as an opportunity to bring her knee up swiftly and violently into his crotch. Bob fell onto the rough sharp gravel of the parking lot. His body writhed with pain. They saw that his face and the skin around his eyes were bleeding. Bob's pale body lay in a fetal position on the ground when Sheriff Cromwell slowly walked onto the scene.

He took his time as he ambled toward Bob, deliberately choosing not to hurry. He stood for a moment and looked down at him with Eden also standing dangerously close. Then the unexpected happened. Sheriff Cromwell's face transformed into a smile and the smile turned into hysterical laughter.

"I wish I could have seen the whole thing."

Bob caught his breath, and his words reflected his shock and embarrassment. "Officer, I want this women arrested for assault. And send an ambulance for me, I think I'm pretty badly hurt. Nancy, get your butt over here and help."

Nancy said simply. "No."

"As I interpret the situation. There are four witnesses to what you say is a crime. I gave you fair warning last night to leave Bear Junction peacefully or you would have me to deal with. Well, this petite woman seemed to take over quite nicely." He started to laugh once again.

"You will be reported to your superiors for your actions."

With a satisfied look, he smiled and stepped back a step to survey the situation. "Mr. Benson, I am the superior. And if I were you, I wouldn't want the word spread about what just occurred in this parking lot. The only way this could have possibly been more enjoyable is if Jerry Anderson was with you. Then you both could have got your asses kicked."

"Sheriff Cromwell, are we going to have to be looking over our shoulders or can you convince him to go back to Rockton?"

"I don't think he is going to want a repeat of what just happened. Besides, I intend to take him down to the station and will be waiting there for you to press charges. No question about it. He did assault Nancy and took her against her will, possibly kidnapping. And as I see it, all you ladies did was protect yourselves. In fact, I witnessed most of it. Are you going to come peacefully, Mr. Benson? Please tell me that you won't. I would enjoy putting you in cuffs."

"Are you crazy? I've been injured. I need medical attention. I don't even think I can walk. Thanks to that crazy bitch."

"Last night it was, I'm too tired. Today it's, I can't walk. I sure hope you'll be able to drive because we sure don't want you in this town any longer than necessary. If you have two brain cells to rub together, I'd give up on this domination kick. It doesn't seem to be working very well for you. Just a suggestion because it doesn't appear that you're a fast learner. If I were you, I wouldn't want to tangle with this little lady again. There isn't much that she's afraid of."

Phyllis smiled. "Just this morning she was afraid of Jake."

Sheriff Cromwell rubbed his forehead and looked at Eden. "I think I'd put my money on her, not the bear."

"Will you stop your fucking yapping and get me some bloody help?"

"Oops, we forgot about your cowardly hide. Sheriff Cromwell, we're not going to press charges. Only because we would have to be here for the court appearance. Besides, it seems my soon-to-be ex-husband got the short end of the stick anyway. Is there anyway that you can assure us that he won't bother us again?"

"I'll go see Judge Pearson and get a restraining order against him for all of you. If he ignores the order, he will be in deep shit." Sheriff Cromwell took Nancy's arm and pulled her aside. "I would like to speak to you about something. I need to inform you of your rights. Your face is already beginning to swell. You will probably have some pretty serious bruises in about an hour. I hope he didn't break any facial bones. Fortunately for you, I witnessed most of the assault. I saw him hit you in the face with such force that you fell to the ground. Look at your arm for God's sake. This man needs to be stopped. I'm going to give you some advice, Mrs. Benson. I realize that Bear Junction is far from your home, but it would be to your advantage to press charges, assault charges. The judge up here doesn't look kindly on men who beat their wives. Another thing, I heard you tell Bob that you intended to divorce him. This assault charge would be a nice little tool. That's all I'm going to say."

"I appreciate your concern sheriff, but I'll recover from my wounds. I always do. I just want to get as far away from that man as I can. I would be more than content with a restraining order. And, I want to thank you for your kindness."

"Keep in mind that he'll be at the police station for a couple hours, in case you change your mind."

"We don't want this little episode to spoil our whole day." Melissa picked up Nancy's purse from the ground and dusted it off.

"It won't. You can be on your way right now. I will have to detain him for a few hours in our local jail. Come on Mr. Benson climb in."

"She just caught me off guard."

"We're going to make sure that you don't get caught off guard again. Why don't you think of it as more for your protection than for hers? Maybe that will make you feel better about the whole situation." It was obvious that the sheriff tried not to laugh again, but he wasn't successful.

Melissa took over her duties as the driver of the Explorer. She spoke as soon as they were out of the parking lot. "Eden, what the hell got into you?"

"I'm sick of him."

"Hope you never get sick of me." Melissa stopped again in front of the drugstore. "Is it safe to get my hair stuff? While I'm in there, I'll get some first aid for Nancy's arm. She tore it up pretty good in the parking lot on that gravel. Nancy, do you think that we're finally through with Bob?"

"Yes. I think he finally realizes that jail would be a very real option. Sheriff Cromwell made that pretty clear. There is only one thing that is as important as his control of me. That's his pristine reputation. Can you imagine how mad he would be if he knew about the tea pot?"

"Or," Melissa added, "The weird charges he's going to find on the credit card. Which, he probably didn't have time to cancel. He's been so busy chasing you around the countryside. Honey, you could have some more fun with that card. After all, we no longer have to worry about Bob tracking us by your charges. Let's get shopping."

When Melissa returned to the drugstore, Nancy became extremely pensive. "Do you know how valuable it is not to live in fear? If I had only one day left on earth, I wouldn't want to live it in fear. Maybe we should all live life like we have only one day left. Phyllis, I've noticed that you've become especially quiet. What's up?"

"I'm still trying to digest what I just witnessed. I could never have been as brave as you and Eden."

"Sure you could, you just have to hit bottom. I kind of

look at my relationship with Bob as a life sentence in prison. If you were serving life, it wouldn't be any big deal to make a break for it. What would I have to lose?"

"You have a strange way with words. I never thought of it in that light. It is kind of a life sentence, isn't it? At night, right before if fall asleep, I force myself to list ten events or thoughts that made me joyful during the day. Sometimes it's so sparse that I have to resort to the sound of an owl or the smell of an orange. Pretty sad, isn't it?"

"Phyllis, you and I were about in the same place. I just decided that I couldn't stand it any more. Maybe you're not quite there yet."

"And maybe I am, but this concept is so new to me. I just haven't thought out the details like you."

Melissa abruptly broke the mood when she opened the door and put her purchases in the back seat with Nancy. "I bought you your goodies. Use that antiseptic cream before your arm gets infected and falls off."

Eden slowly laid her head against the back of the seat. "Melissa, will you drive past that antique store?"

TWENTY-FIVE

There it is, on the corner. Now this is the second time you've dragged me back. When the hell are you going to get over it? I suppose you want me to stop again. No big deal, there's lots of places to park." Melissa parked the Explorer directly in front of the storefront, being careful to notice there were no restrictions. "Jump out and look in the window. You know you won't be happy until you do."

Eden didn't hesitate. As she flew out of the vehicle, she looked once again through the small glass window in the front of the shop. She was disappointed that nothing changed from the last time. The large gold leafed mirror was right where she last saw it and the rest of the antique shop was vacant. It took only a minute and she returned to her seat in the Explorer. They proceeded through the town and onto the highway headed for Cranston.

"Melissa, was this a figment of our vivid imaginations? Phyllis, do you know anything about that antique shop?"

"What shop? I don't recall ever seeing an antique shop on this corner. In fact, I don't remember anything ever being here. Eden, why don't you tell me what's bugging you?"

"Melissa and I visited an antique shop that was in this building. It was in the afternoon. It was filled to the brim with wonderful antiques. There was an impressive humungous mirror and a lot of large heavy carved furniture. I spoke with the most unusual man, who told me things that he had no way of knowing. The next morning Melissa and I returned to find it bare to the bones. The only item left was that large gold mirror. Melissa swears up and down that he and I were speaking French together, but don't speak a word of French." Eden paused for a couple of minutes before she began to talk again. "I'm a realist. There has to be an answer that is logical, but I sure can't come up with it. We both know that there is no magic or ghosts. If Melissa and I both hadn't experienced the same thing, I would have thought I was delusional."

"I have a lot of acquaintances in Bear Junction. Do you want me to look into it for you?"

Nancy chimed in. "Bear Junction is a strange place. It has no warmth and it reeks of an odd energy. I learned a long time ago that for some things, there are no answers."

"Of course, there are answers. There are answers for everything. It just isn't obvious. There is more to this than just a fast move. Maybe he hired a good moving team. Maybe he didn't pay his rent and had to move in the middle of the night. What did he say to you?"

"No, not a good moving team, Phyllis. You didn't see the enormity of that shop. It would have been impossible. Besides, let's get real. This is Bear Junction. Where would he hire twenty men and ten trucks to move him in the middle of the night? He knew that I was a Scorpio, which was shocking enough. But he told me that life on earth was a school house, and that I was going to learn a life lesson that would be life shattering, definitely not pleasant. I can't remember word for word but...." Her words trailed off, making her voice become inaudible.

Melissa looked at Eden. "Daa, that's because you were speaking French."

"I've told you at least ten times that I speak English and Spanish. Not French. You're dead wrong, Melissa."

"He spoke kind of old world and dressed formally. He wasn't attractive in the least. In fact, he looked like Orson Wells. He told me that my trip to Bear Junction was the most important journey of my life. And that I'll take something from here that will change my life forever. He warned me that if I wasn't ready that I should get out of here quickly."

"For somebody who didn't remember it all it ....."

"I told you before, I have a photographic memory." Eden became annoyed. "If I sound like a broken record, it's because I've never had anything so strange happen to me."

Nancy spoke loudly. "Melissa, pull over in the next driveway and turn around."

"What are you talking about, honey?"

"We're going back to Bear Junction. Let's hurry before Sheriff Cromwell lets him go. I've decided to pull the plug on this Bob thing once and for all. I am going to press charges. The sheriff was right."

Eden took her camera from the glove box. "We need to take pictures of your arm. As soon as you have the full-blown bruises on your face, we'll get pictures of that, too. Good girl. I know you're upset about coming back here, but don't be. We'll be with you. With the pictures and the criminal charge over his head, you can be sure that Bob won't be bullying you in divorce court. He'll want to keep what happened today hush hush. I can't imagine that he'd want anybody in his insulated little world to find out."

The squad car was parked in front of the police station. "Thank God, he's still here." Melissa parked the Explorer on the side of the unpretentious building. "Won't Bob be surprised to see his unexpected guests?"

"Yes, he's used to having everything his way. I guess, as of now, that I'm officially in charge."

Sheriff Cromwell didn't see them approach the building as he was checking something that he had attached to a clipboard. His face gave way to a surprised expression when he saw the four women walk up to him.

"Did you forget something?"

"Yes, I forgot to press charges against Bob Benson."

"Well, in that case, I'm glad you remembered. Come on in, and let's get this show on the road. I was on my way over to the courthouse to get the restraining order in process. I'll start the paperwork and then go over to the drugstore and get a sworn statement from Violet Warner. You told me that she saw Mr. Benson drag you out the back door?"

"Right. Is this going to take a long time? Not that I mind, of course."

"Nancy, you will need to sign a few papers to get the ball rolling. You can leave and come back about four to finish up. Trust me, the modest bit of inconvenience that you're going through is nothing to what Bob Benson is going to experience." He laughed his infectious laugh which made the four women join in.

"Sheriff Cromwell, whatever happened to that antique store on the corner of Main Street and Rome Avenue?"

"Phyllis, I don't remember any antique shop there. That would be next to Milly's flower shop. I don't think there's been anything there for years. All the locals think the place is haunted so Jim Miller has had a hard time renting it for any price. He can't even give it away."

Melissa's eyes got big. "Haunted, why do they think it haunted?"

"It's got a reputation. Well, just say that lots of tall tales have come out of the bar, Carl's Place. After a few drinks, the stories get bigger and a hell of a lot more interesting. I've heard those tales ever since I was a kid. I try not to get too involved in that kind of crazy stuff. But that sure doesn't change the fact that Jim can't seem to rent it or sell it."

"Could it be possible that it was rented as an antique shop, and the proprietors moved in the middle of the night?"

"Not likely. Jim Miller was complaining to me about a month ago that he didn't know what to do with it. It's on Main Street. I am up and down that street a hundred times a day and night too. Don't get me going on that, I'm a cop not a ghost buster." He hesitated for a minute. "Please don't tell me you have some weird story about that place."

It took only a half hour to get the paperwork started. Nancy promised that they would be back at three or four to finish it and learn what the next step was. Finally they were headed to Cranston for a day of shopping and lunching.

Phyllis wistfully watched the scenery unfold as the Explorer wound its way through wooded country roads. "What am I going to do for excitement after you leave?"

Nancy wasn't sure how far she was prepared to go with this conversation. "Phyllis, I promise that we won't leave without telling you the reason for our trip."

"The reason was to hide from Bob, wasn't it? Although I did wonder why it was necessary to come disguised."

"Please do yourself a favor and don't give it too much thought right now. I made you a promise that I intend to keep. Just be patient, you'll learn everything soon enough."

For a tiny town, Cranston was bustling, mostly with middle-aged ladies carrying packages and shopping bags. "Melissa, turn left at the next street. There's good parking, and it's close to that restaurant that I told you about. There it is and it's open. Eden, it's pretty expensive. Are you sure you're up to it?"

"Yes, she's up to it." Melissa volunteered. "There's a darling boutique. In fact it's called Darling Boutique. Get that credit card out, Nancy, you're going to wear it thin today. You're going to need some new clothes for your new job."

"What new job?"

"The one you're going to get wearing your new clothes." Melissa was already out of the Explorer and pulling Nancy down the street. "*Darling Boutique* is a hole in the wall, but a pretty elegant hole in the wall."

"I don't know about this place, Melissa. It's pretty fancy for my taste. You are so wild."

Melissa began to dance down the sidewalk, singing at the top of her lungs. "Wild thing, you make my heart sing."

The two elderly ladies that she danced past turned around and starred at her. One of them said something behind her hand. Melissa finally stopped her crazy antics.

"Seems to me that your tastes have changed in the last week or so. Remember, you left the old Nancy back in Rockton." Melissa took a slinky black silk dress off the hanger and stuffed it into Nancy's hands. "Try this on. It'll be great for those wonderful sexy Chicago nights. It will be absolutely perfect for your new blonde image."

Nancy also took a more conservative summer suit with her into the changing room. "I need some office clothes. It didn't matter in the insurance office in Rockton, but Chicago will be another story."

Eden put her hand on Nancy's shoulder. "I want you to look at the facts realistically. Nancy, you will soon be half owner of Benson Insurance Agency and the house. Don't sell yourself short. You'll have enough money from the divorce to open your own agency. I know you have as much knowledge as Bob. All you need is your license. With all your experience, you should buzz right through that exam. You were the backbone of that business. It's time you looked at the big picture."

Nancy's mouth hung open, as she looked at Eden awestruck.

TWENTY-SIX

To Nancy's delight, the beautiful, shiny, golden credit card had not been canceled. Within three hours she bought five outfits, plus the slinky black dress for sexy Chicago nights. She also purchased two necklaces, three pair of earrings, several sets of new underwear, a swimsuit, hose, two purses, a lightweight coat, a blue cashmere sweater, and four pairs of shoes.

"Whew, shopping is hard work." Nancy opened the door of the restaurant for her friends. "Eden, I'm starved. You might be sorry that you offered to pay."

"I'm sure I will." She laughed. "Nancy, how long has it been since you bought anything nice for yourself? I mean something really special."

"Hmmm. A lifetime ago."

The restraunt was a pleasant surprise. It was a woman's kind of place. The building was Victorian with high ceilings and cove moldings. The lace curtains were held back with silk rosebud. The tables were set with white tableclothes, candles, and fresh flowers. Eden disappeared for a minute to use the bathroom. When Nancy turned around, she saw her in deep conversation with the owner.

Melissa ordered seafood bisque to start. Everybody

laughed at the outrageous prices, even Eden, who was the victim smiled and shook her head. The meal's dialogue was light and happy, which didn't include any of the fiasco in the drugstore parking lot. Melissa sat facing the window with her back to the restaurant. She saw the waitress approach carrying an elaborately decorated birthday cake. She looked at her three smiling friends unable to control the two stray tears that ran down her cheeks.

Nancy gently patted Melissa's hand. "This is the best part of my day to see you so happy. But I sure wish you wouldn't cry. You're going to get us all going." She handed Melissa a bag that came from one of the boutiques. "Didn't have time to wrap it. This is from the three of us."

Melissa pulled out a beautiful cream and red print silk dress that she fell in love with in one of the high-end stores. She encouraged Nancy to buy it. "This was supposed to be for your new life."

"We all saw how much you loved it and decided it would be for your new life."

"Honey, I don't have a new life. I'm stuck with the old one, which isn't all that bad."

Nancy cut the cake while Eden took another bite of her raspberry chicken salad. "Whatever happened to, one for all and all for one? Remember, the three musketeers? I wish you would consider coming to Chicago, at least until we get Nancy on her feet. Nancy has always looked to you as her tower of strength. We lost each other for so many years. Let's not split up again. Unless there's something in Rockton that you're not telling me about, why don't you move with Nancy to Chicago? I can get work for both of you in my company. Or, if you insist on remaining a waitress, I can help there, too. What do you say, Melissa? You two can stay with me in Oak Park until you start earning enough money fly out of the nest and get an apartment. Victor, as grumpy as he is, would love it."

Phyllis, who was enthralled with the conversation, couldn't resist breaking in. "Eden, is Victor your husband or boyfriend?"

"Thank God, neither. He's annoying, fat, and obnoxious. If he were human, he would probably still be annoying, fat, and obnoxious. We would have been in the divorce courts years ago."

Phyllis frowned. "What is he, a Martian?"

"He might just as well be. I wouldn't doubt it. Phyllis, Victor's a big, gray, tabby cat who thinks he's heir to the throne."

"This cake is wonderful. How did you know that I love lemon filling. That's my favorite." Melissa discreetly pushed a sugar rose off the top of her piece and maneuvered it to the side of her plate with her fork. She took a deep breath and hesitated before she spoke. "Phyllis, I'll go if you go."

"Melissa, you're so nonchalant about this life changing decision. Jerry would be lost without me. I don't know how he'd survive." She studied her half eaten slice of cake with downcast eyes.

Eden gave Nancy a sly smile. "It's just food for thought. Think about it but don't dismiss the idea. We're not nearly done with you yet."

"What do you mean by that? You girls keep alluding to something. I don't half understand what you're talking about."

"You're not meant to, not yet. Don't spend this incredible day trying to figure it out. We gave you our word that you wouldn't be left in the dark and the three musketeers never break their promises." Eden promptly changed the subject. "When we go back to Bear Junction to see Sheriff Cromwell, do you mind if we have a quick drink at Carl's Place? Now I am even more curious about that antique shop."

"You know, Eden, you're beginning to creep me out. You can't seem to let go of this can you? I've got to admit that I'm kind of fascinated, too. I've never seen a ghost or knew anybody who had."

Eden lifted her coffee cup. "I want to propose a toast. Here's to Melissa and to many more of her happy birthdays. And here's to Nancy and Phyllis and fantastic changes that are predestined to be made."

"Enough of the serious stuff, we have more important things to do." Melissa looked at her well-worn watch. "As I see it, we've got about an hour and a half of good shopping time left."

Phyllis put up her hand in a stop position. "No, I can't shop another minute. I'm so full from this magnificent lunch. And to be honest, my feet are killing me. Keep in mind that I've got about twenty years on you girls. You need to take pity on my poor old decrepit body. Why don't you shop your hearts, out and I'll sit here and watch the people? I'm going to order a pot of tea and have a nice reflective time by myself."

Nancy smiled at Melissa. "Be off with you. Tea and quiet time sounds nice, too. I'll stay with Phyllis if you don't mind."

Eden generously paid the bill, which included a substantial tip. She stopped their waitress on their way out. Motioning to the rear of the room. "Where does that lovely back door go?"

"There's a small English garden with a couple umbrella tables."

"My friends over there think we're going shopping. Can you serve us coffee out there, and let us all hang out for about an hour? If you get busy and need the tables, let us know." Eden slipped her a fifty-dollar bill.

"Yes, of course. And I won't be telling them where you are."

"I'm so grateful that I don't have to see one more cutesy shop. Wasn't Nancy clever to be able to spend some more time with Phyllis? She seems to listen to Nancy. Even when one of us says exactly the same thing, Phyllis digs in her heels. I think she'll come around, but she still needs some more time."

"This is a refreshing shock. Who would have thought that this tiny village had a garden straight from a picture out of an English coffee table book? Look it even has fox gloves."

"Where's Angela Lansbury?"

"Melissa, I need to make a couple phone calls. I need to talk to my housekeeper and to Justin at the office. Then be prepared, I think we should talk about your future life after Wilderness Lodge."

"Can't we just play it by ear?"

"No." Eden said simply and then dialed her cell phone.

Phyllis and Nancy sat comfortably with a pot of tea between them. "Nancy, aren't you just a little scared of what the future is going to hold? Your life in Chicago will be so different than what you were used to in Rockton."

"No, I'm extremely excited. Everyday will be a new adventure. You know, this is a foreign way of thinking for me. Adventure was never in my vocabulary. I'm happier than I ever remember, even as a child."

"What was your childhood like?"

"Trust me, you don't want to hear about my sad, pathetic childhood."

"Nancy, I didn't want to upset you at lunch, but your face isn't swollen anymore. There is a huge bruise and your left eye is black and blue. I'm sorry. I think it's time to take pictures."

Nancy didn't seem upset at Phyllis' observation. She lightly touched the swollen part of her face with her fingertips. Her voice dropped to a whisper. "Good, the noose tightens around old Bob Benson's neck."

"Has Bob ever hurt you before?"

"Of course, but never in front of witnesses or in a part of my body that wasn't covered by clothes. This one will be a costly mistake."

"How about you?"

"Yes, but Jerry is a lot like Bob, never in front of witnesses. No matter how drunk Jerry gets, at least he keeps his composure until we're in private. One thing about Jerry, at least he doesn't humiliate me in front of anybody."

"Phyllis, that doesn't make him thoughtful and kind. It just makes him clever. I wish that you could understand that. When I see you and Jerry together, I can't see the love and I can't feel the love. Was it there between Jerry and your daughter? Are we good enough friends yet, that you can discuss his relationship with your daughter?"

"It's so painful. But I guess that I'm ready to talk about it. It's all the things that we try to hide and conceal that torment us. Paula hates her father and that's a fact. I'm a coward. I have never wanted to know the reason. No details for me. That's my mantra. I have always been afraid that if I knew the true basis on why she hated him, I would have to take some kind of action. There were a couple of times when she was younger that she seemed to need to talk about it. I hushed her. I told her that I would not stand for her to be disrespectful to Jerry. I told myself that the reason she disliked him was that he was a strict father and that no child or young adult likes authority."

"It's only the two of us sitting at this table. In retrospect, what do you think? Over the years, did you ever have any thoughts or suspicions?"

"I told Jerry that if I ever suspected abuse or saw bruises on her, our marriage would be over. I meant it. I believed in my heart that it was okay to abuse me but not acceptable to abuse Paula."

"You know that hitting is only one kind of abuse and it's, by far, not the most permanent."

"Nancy, what are you saying? Are you trying to plant a seed in my mind? Are you speaking this way because your father abused you?"

"No, Phyllis, my father didn't abuse me, not ever. In fact, that's the second time that I've answered that question in the past week. If you want to, let's not talk about your daughter anymore. I'm getting the feeling that you're uncomfortable with that subject. I guess I'm confused. We both know that I can't plant a seed in soil that is not fertile."

TWENTY-SEVEN

I'm glad that's over." Nancy walked briskly down the cement sidewalk from the police station to the Explorer. "It's a good thing that Eden forced me to take pictures of my face and arm."

"Well, Nancy, it sounds like we'll be coming back here in a month." Eden climbed into the driver's seat and started the engine. "In other words we have a month to find a superior divorce attorney for you. These two events should be consecutive."

Melissa laughed. "Eden, if you don't stop talking with those big words, I'm going to sing "Wild Thing" and dance through the police station."

"Melissa, you're four cents short of a nickel. Let's get out of here before you find yourself sharing a cell with Bob."

"Speaking of Bob, Sheriff Cromwell let him leave a couple of hours ago. I hope the idiot had the good sense to get out of town." Nancy looked troubled "You don't suppose that he ...."

"Wish he would," Melissa said. "That would be the last nail in his coffin. hat are you doing? Eden, you were serious about going to Carl's Place?"

"We won't stay very long. He'll have time to talk to us, the parking lot is nearly empty. It's even too early for the hard core drinkers."

Carl was behind the bar drying glasses when they entered. Melissa whispered to Eden. "Which is shinier, the bar glasses or his bald head? The reflection is going to blind me."

"Hullo, ladies, what can I do you for?" Carl had a pronounced split between his two front teeth. He picked up a white bar towel and began to wipe the bar in front of them.

"How about a glass of red wine for each of us." Eden whipped a twenty out of her purse and laid it down. She thought about how difficult it would be to concentrate on what Carl was going to say. She couldn't take her eyes off his mustache. Some people hardly moved their upper lip while talking, which would not be Carl. His mustache looked like a piece of animated steel wool.

The other man who sat at the bar was about fifty. He wore a faded blue tee shirt that held his cigarette package in one of the sleeves. "Phyllis, good to see you. I hope Jerry isn't too mad at me for not coming out to fix his boat. I wasn't about to get blown into the lake in that damn storm."

"If Jerry is mad about that, he's the one with the problem. He'll just have to get over it. Jim, these are guests at the lodge, Eden, Melissa, and Nancy. They're from Illinois. This is Jim Carver and Carl Baumgartner."

Carl laughed, "Eden, eh, like the garden of Eden?" The split between his teeth became the focal point as he hissed like a snake.

Eden ignored his attempt at humor and the strong urge to kick him in the crotch. As usual, she got right to the point. "Have you guys lived in Bear Junction for a long time?"

"Carl and I have lived here all our lives, born, bred, and raised." Carl gave him another glass of beer.

"I'm curious about something. Tell me what you know about that building on the corner of Main Street and Rome Avenue. Do you know anything about an antique store that was there?"

Carl laughed hardily. "You came to the right place to hear those stories. Jim's in his glory telling them, good at it, too. You better order another drink cause he's not likely to shut up for hours."

"Jim, we don't have hours, will you give us the *Readers Digest* condensed version?"

"Are you here to rent that store?"

"No, nothing like that. We're just curious about why it's such a sore subject with the local people. Melissa and I could have sworn we saw an antique shop there."

Jim took one last puff on his cigarette before he snuffed it in the dirty ashtray. Not likely. The last thing in that store was a gift shop that was run by a couple of sisters from Madison. It was probably about ten years ago. Carl, wasn't it about ten or twelve years ago?

Yea, my wife went there once after they opened it. The women here wouldn't go there alone, she went with three or four of her friends. That place is pretty weird. They just rented it, they didn't buy it. It's a good thing for them because they sure didn't last long."

Eden looked puzzled. "Are they the people who left the big mirror?"

"No, that mirror has always been there. It's too big to

move. That mirror was there when I was a little boy. Anyway, those women stayed just a few months. It was a nice little set up they had. Marion, the older sister, had a breakdown and tried to kill herself. Karen, the other one, took her back to Madison. When she came back, she had one hell of a sale like this town has never seen. She wanted out of here quick so she sold all the stuff so cheap you couldn't believe it. Neither could my wife. We've got more fu fu crap than we know what to do with. The rumors really flew when Marion had that nervous breakdown. They say that it was the ghost that drove her over the edge."

Phyllis looked thoughtful. "I heard that the so called ghost is a man and that he's been seen by more than just a few people over the years. When did this thing start?"

"Hell, I don't know. A long time ago, maybe even a hundred years ago. Who knows how much of this is real and how much of it comes out of a whiskey bottle? The weird thing is everybody through the years describe him the same."

Eden interrupted. "Portly and well dressed, with some kind of a foreign accent?"

"Heavy and well dressed, he even has a pocket watch. A lot more than an accent, honey. The guy speaks French, and nobody can understand a word he says. But, hell, nobody hangs around long enough to listen to him either. The rumor has always been in Bear Junction, and I don't know anybody who knows how the whole thing got started."

Phyllis pushed her half empty wine glass aside. "If you girls want a swim before dinner, we better get going.

All this ghost business is making the hair on the back of my neck stand up."

"You saw him, didn't you?"

"Melissa and I both saw him, plus I spoke with him."

"You speak French?"

"No, not a word. But for some reason Melissa said that I was speaking French with him. I have a hard time believing that. When we went back the next morning, all the antiques were gone. The only thing familiar was the gold mirror."

The drive back to Wilderness Lodge seemed to take longer than usual. "Eden, are you glad you had a chance to talk to Carl and Jim?"

"Not particularly. I guess I didn't want what I suspected, confirmed."

Eden stopped the Explorer in front of the lodge to drop off Phyllis. "You better use the repellent. This time of the day is the worst for mosquitos and those biting flies. Anybody hungry? I thought I would just serve sandwiches and chips tonight. is that okay?"

"Perfect. If you have time come down to the lake and join us." Eden waved as she walked into the lodge. "What do you want to bet that Jerry will make her cook a huge dinner? It'll be her punishment for being gone all day."

They decided it was too late to swim. The wind was picking up and the lake air was becoming cool. Knowing the water would be like ice, they thought a walk on the beach would be more enjoyable than a frigid swim. The declining sun turned the lake into molten gold.

Melissa carried her shoes and went ankle deep into the water. "We made a great choice. This water is frigging freezing. Besides, swimming wasn't the real reason we're down here. Tonight's the biggy and we better make some serious plans. Did you make any headway with Phyllis at lunch, Nancy?"

"Just reinforcement. Yes, I nearly got her to admit that Jerry was abusive with their daughter, Paula. She told me that she closed her ears to her daughter. Phyllis was definitely in denial while Paula was growing up. In fact, I think she's still in denial. God only knows how she is going to react when we tell her about Jerry. At least we won't have to contend with Gene and Les. They're going to eat in town. I hope our buddy, Jerry, goes to bed early. If not, we may be stuck here another day. I can't believe how many life changing events have occurred in such a short span of time." Nancy sat on a big gray rock and looked at the beautiful sunset. "Part of me dreads tonight and another part is anxious to get it over with I hope Jerry got a head start on his drinking while we were in town. Not that he needs any excuses."

Melissa found the water uncomfortably cold on her feet as her ankles began to ache with the icy water's assault. The shore was not nice, soft, fine sand. It was course stone that cut into her soles. She sat down and buckled her sandals.

"How are we going to do it? It's not going to be an 'oh by the way' type of conversation. Should we be painfully blunt or should we candy coat it? I wish I knew how Phyllis was going to react. It won't be a pretty sight. She is such a good person, I almost hate laying this on her. I know one thing for sure, this is going to have to be a group effort. It will have to be the three of us together. I hate to say it, it's my worst nightmare but I'm willing to stay another day or two if I have to. We've come way too far to blow it now."

"Let's not go up to the lodge until we absolutely have to. The fewer minutes we have to spend with Jerry the better. Under no circumstances let that ass hole goad us into admitting that we remember the way he molested us. I don't care how many lies we have to tell. We better keep our cool. Let's not lock horns with him. We're going to have to keep it peaceful so he goes to bed early. If we get him riled up, it could be hours of arguing. We all know that after a few drinks, that's his favorite sport."

"Eden, your photographic memory just shrunk. Do you really want to be walking along this beach at night after our encounter with Jake?" Nancy was already heading up the incline to the lodge, not waiting for Eden's reply. I hope you still have that revolver in your purse. I have a strange premonition about tonight, and it doesn't sit well."

Eden had to run to keep up. The terrain felt so uneven under her feet she was in danger of falling. The weeds along the incline popped up in unexpected places. "You know that we risk him bringing up the molestations."

Those words of Eden's stopped Nancy in her tracks. She whirled around and looked Eden in the eyes. "Oh, my God, maybe we made a mistake not telling Phyllis this afternoon. We had her out of town where she couldn't have escaped."

Melissa finally caught up. "Exactly, but as I see it we can't cry over spilled milk. It's all a gamble, but we need to continue with our plan. I always look at things in the negative. I ask myself. What's the worst thing that can happen? In this particular case, the worst thing would be Jerry confronting our intentions." She flicked away a mosquito with her hand. "This damn bug repellent is acting like a spice for their food." She continued. "This afternoon is gone. If things get too difficult with Jerry, we'll just have to leave and go to our cabin. We'll have to start again tomorrow with a clean slate."

"Which one of us is going to make that decision? I say Eden."

Eden's was a mouth that could tighten into a fine line. "I'm tired of being the head of this dragon."

"Shut up, Eden, we know how you love being in charge." Melissa playfully put her arm around her as they climbed the slope together toward Wilderness Lodge.

TWENTY-EIGHT

The first sight the three women had when the walked through the door of the lodge was Jerry. A morose figure at his usual place at the end of the bar, as he smoked his habitual, foul smelling cigar.

Eden spoke just loud enough for Melissa and Nancy to hear. "And let the games begin."

He yelled across the room. "How about a drink? Phyllis isn't quite done in the kitchen. She decided to make a big spaghetti dinner."

Melissa whispered. "Yea, I'll just bet she did."

"I watched you out the back window. In fact, I was all ready to go find the binoculars. I thought you ladies were going to go for a swim. I was definitely disappointed. My old eyes were all conditioned to seeing three beautiful women parading up and down the beach in skimpy bikinis. No nerve? What's the matter, that nice Lake Superior water was a little cool for you?" He laughed a cynical loud laugh. "Have those heated pools made you soft?"

Nancy discreetly pinched Eden's arm. "Be pleasant, remember?"

"No, Jerry, we decided that we just wanted to enjoy that glorious golden sunset. We don't get many of those in Illinois." Nancy led the threesome to the bar. "We had a big lunch, sandwiches and chips would have been perfect. Phyllis seemed a little tired by the time we got back."

"Life isn't always about getting what we want, is it? Don't worry about Phyllis. That woman loves to cook. "He swiveled his barstool to better face them. "So many years ago, but I believe I remember you ladies from Rockton Grade School."

He looked from one to the other of the three friends. He smiled, giving them an unappreciated view of his cigar yellowed teeth. Jerry waited unwearyingly for their response.

"As a matter of fact, we were just talking about that on the beach." Eden and Nancy gazed at Melissa in stupefied silence. Both held their breath in anticipation of her next ill-advised words. "It was kind of strange but a lot of grade school was blocked from our memories. I remember you teaching the other third grade class. We had Mrs. Mason as our teacher. I'm surprised that you even remember us."

"How could I ever forget such sweet little girls?" He had a wicked glint in his eye.

Melissa fought the urge to lunge at him, but she was comforted by the fact that they would soon have their sweet revenge. Melissa knew that he was trying to bait them, but it didn't make the situation easier. She could tell that he was enjoying it, like he was playing a game. Almost like a predator stalking its victim. He looked up and down their bodies as though he was undressing each of them.

It was an enormous relief when Phyllis poked her head into the bar area. "Are you ready for spaghetti and meatballs. It's all dished up and ready."

"It sounds wonderful." Eden said dishonestly. "We're kind of half planning on leaving in the morning, but nothing is still for certain."

Jerry spoke sarcastically. "You must either have a great job or where they don't care when or if you ever come back." He looked at her intently, in anticipation of her answer.

Eden's fists clenched under the checkered tablecloth. "The earmark of a good leader is to be content that all is working well in her absence." She nonchalantly took a small bite of her garlic bread, giving the impression of dismissal.

Nancy thought she was going to vomit. Feelings of stress always had that effect on her stomach, like they did at so many meal times with Bob. She took a deep breath and a long sip of her iced water. Nancy decided that never again would any man have the power to make her throw up. "Did you work on your boat today? It's too bad that we didn't have the chance to go out on the lake while we were here."

"Something strange about that motor. Jim came out here this afternoon after he saw you in town. We worked on it for about an hour. Neither one of us can figure out how it got in that screwed up condition. If I didn't know better, I'd say it was tampered with."

Melissa laughed, she couldn't help it. "I always say,

don't ever trust teenagers or Jake with a pair of pliers."

"You don't take too much very seriously, do you Melissa?"

"That's where you're wrong, Mr. Anderson."

Eden looked at Melissa and wished that she could stuff her mouth with something. Anything to shut her up. Please, dear God, Eden thought, don't let her play into Jerry's hand. It was so obvious to Eden that she was being baited.

Eden forced a smile. "Phyllis, if I cooked, I'd ask you for your recipe for this delicious spaghetti sauce."

"Yea, you don't look like the type who could boil water." Jerry had his mouth half full of food, displaying half the contents.

Melissa looked at Nancy's face begin to pale. She knew that she was about ready for a trip to the bathroom. "Eden might not be able to boil water, but she makes a hell of a margarita. Besides, Eden has enough money to pay others to cook for her. So tell us, what did you do today?"

"I thought I already told you, you must not be listening. I worked my ass off on that boat engine. And might I add, it still isn't right. It seems as though it's missing an integral part. Jim seems to think that it fell off and is at the bottom of the lake, although I'm not so sure. It's ordered and will be here in a few days."

"Out all day in that sun and air must take its toll. I'll bet you're exhausted." A bit too obvious, Eden thought.

"No, I'm used to it. I live here, remember? Jim told me

that you were pumping him for information about the store at Main and Rome." He laughed. "I guess I give you too much credit. I thought you were smarter than to listen to the ramblings of stupid, uneducated trailer trash."

"Jerry, being it's probably going to be the girls' last night here, do you think we can break out that good bottle of French wine?"

"Sure, why not?" He pushed back his chair from the table without sliding it back in. "I'll go get it while you women clean up the mess."

On their way to the kitchen, Melissa said to Nancy. "I didn't think I could hate him more than I did, but I was wrong. Jerry always seems to sink to an all new low. He's really a pathetic shell of a man."

"Melissa, if you don't forgive someone, it's like taking poison and hoping your enemy will die."

Melissa hit her in the arm. "Nancy, no more sermons. This is not the time or the place. I know that Eden's probably most worried about me screwing things up with my temper, but she should be more worried about you. I'm warning you Nancy, you damned better not go soft on us."

"I'd feel a lot more comfortable if we had a plan."

"How could we possibly have a plan? Jerry is a loose cannon. Tell me, how can we make our plans around a mad man?"

Seated at the bar, Melissa pointed at the TV. "Are we finally going to watch Letterman tonight?"

"What's with you women and Letterman? He's a big waste of time."

"Jerry can't stand him. I usually sit here by myself in the evening watching TV."

"He's my favorite." Eden lied. "Hopefully, he'll have a good show tonight."

Jerry popped the cork in the wine bottle. "Well, we've got a half hour before he comes on, let's all enjoy a glass of this good wine. We were saving it for a celebration, but I guess this will do." He stood with his back to the bar as he poured everyone a generous glass of the wine. Jerry slid the glasses in front of everybody and raised his in a toast. "Here's to a safe and uneventful trip home."

"Thank you, Jerry. But like I said earlier, tomorrow might not be the day we leave. It's possible that you're stuck with us another day."

"Okay, I forgot. Red wine has an effect on my eyelids. I'm glad I don't have to drive anywhere to get home. I used to be able to stay up half the night. I must be letting my age get the best of me." He stretched. "Look at me, it's only nine thirty and I'm beat." Without another word he walked behind the bar.

Eden decided that she needed a clear head for what was about to transpire, so she took only a small sip of her wine in the toast. "Please", she thought, "go to bed and let us get on with the messy job of telling Phyllis about your sick transgressions."

When Jerry finished his wine, he opened another

bottle and set it in front of Phyllis. "Here, it isn't as good as that French stuff, but enjoy. If you ladies will excuse me, I need my beauty sleep."

The three friends thought it was out of character for Jerry to be so accommodating, but gratefully dismissed it from their minds. Both Melissa and Nancy finished their wine. Phyllis refilled their glasses from the bottle that Jerry opened.

Nancy took a sip and commented. "This isn't too bad."

Phyllis took the channel changer, but Nancy gently slid it from her hand and pressed the off button. She looked from Eden to Melissa who gave her a silent affirmation. Phyllis looked at her in surprise.

"Letterman isn't on our agenda for tonight." She stood and took her glass and the wine bottle, motioning for Phyllis to follow them to one of the small dining tables. "This is the moment that we've dreaded all week, but it has to be said."

"I knew there was something wrong. I would have had to been a fool not to have known there was something in the wind. Look, maybe I want life to go on as it is. I might not want to know what you have to tell me. It's not too late, Nancy."

Eden's wine glass wasn't quite half empty. She took another sip. "I'm glad you enjoyed this wine, but I think I'm going to pour mine out and get a Coke. I'm not in the mood for wine." She went quickly to the bar and retrieved a soda. "Nancy, before we met you we hoped you were a monster. But we have grown to love you like a sister. In fact, in a strange perverse way, we all are sisters."

"You're making me nervous. Please get on with whatever you seem so determined to tell me."

Melissa patted Nancy's hand. She took a deep breath and began. "Honey, we're not on vacation. We had a purpose for coming here. We haven't seen Eden in years and connected after a Rockton high school reunion. Nancy and I spent the weekend with her in Oak Park. We all had a horrible secret."

"No, no. I don't want to hear anymore." Phyllis put her hands over her ears. Melissa compassionately pulled her hands down to the table. "No more denial. You have a good idea what this is about, don't you?"

"Melissa, let me." Nancy paused a moment and began again. "Phyllis, we're not here to have a pity party. We're here to free you, the truth will set you free." Nancy looked to Eden for support but she was daydreaming, with her mouth slightly ajar.

"I know what you're doing, and I'm too old to walk off into the sunset with just the clothes on my back." A tear rolled down her cheek, and she wiped it away with the pad of her thumb. "I know Jerry is a nasty, unpleasant alcoholic, but many people have chosen to live with that kind of a spouse. I don't have the strength to make a change."

Melissa began again. "If he was just a drunk…. no, honey, it's so much more than that. We came to Wilderness Lodge to confront our demons. Jerry is our demon. He molested three innocent little girls in the third grade. We were those little girls." Melissa looked at Eden who didn't seem aware of what was transpiring. She then looked at Nancy who was gazing at Eden with a puzzled look on her face. "Eden, we're counting on you for some support. What's wrong with you? You're never at a loss for words."

Eden slowly stood. "I'm exhausted. If I don't get back to the cabin, I'm going to fall asleep right here."

"Are you okay? You don't look quite right."

"Sure, just try not to wake me when you come back. I'm sorry, I wanted to be part of this. I don't know what got into me." She picked up her purse and slowly walked toward the door. "Will you watch out the window to make sure Jake doesn't eat me?"

They watched from their table to make certain that Eden made it safely to the cabin.

"Something isn't right." Melissa stood and started to take a step toward the door.

"Sit down, Melissa, we need you here more than Eden."

Phyllis took the news without hysteria or massive tears. "I think poor Phyllis is in shock." Nancy said to Melissa. "We came here to hunt him down. We left Oak Park without a plan and when we got here we realized that nothing we could do would make him a more miserable human being. In reality, he's already dead."

Melissa put her arm around Phyllis' shoulders.

"Honey, it's not too late for us to save you. Come back to Oak Park with us. Nancy and I are going to start over, why not one more? Eden will be there to support us 'til we get on our feet, she promised. Phyllis, Eden's a good person."

"How could Jerry have molested you? We were married. So far, you haven't shown me any proof of that, prove it if you want me to believe you. Prove it. I want some proof. You three could be lying. This could be a crazy evil lie that you just made up."

"For what reason? Why would we drive to this God forsaken place and waste a week of our lives to tell you this horrendous elaborate lie? What can we possibly tell you to prove what we just told you?" Nancy silently thought for a few moments "I know, we'll describe the inside of your house. Tell her, Melissa, tell her about the towels we used in their bathroom to clean up after his dirty deeds."

Melissa gave Nancy a shocked look. "Okay, I'll tell her. They were white…they were white with beautiful little pink rose buds. Isn't that ironic? You had a breadbox in the kitchen and sometimes if we were good little girls, he would give us a cookie out of that painted green breadbox. I would always go home and throw up that cookie. They were usually peanut butter and to this day I can't eat a peanut butter cookie. We did what he said and kept our mouths shut because he threatened to kill our families with that big knife that you kept in the drawer to the left of the sink. You were never home, you worked somewhere in Rockford."

They sat in silence for what seemed to be an extremely long amount of time. Phyllis could be heard taking deep breaths. God, thought Nancy, I wish I could figure out what's going on in her head. Phyllis spoke in a voice that was barely audible. "I'm going to kill him."

"No you're not." Nancy pulled on her wrist to seat her once again in her chair. "We talked about that option and decided that he's already dead. We would end up in prison. My question to you is, do any of us deserve to be further punished? Please sit and talk to us. When we're talked out, you're going to spend the night in our cabin. Or, if you'd prefer, we'll pack up and spend the night at the motel in Bear Junction. Or better yet, head for Chicago. It's your call. We've given you way too much for you to comprehend in one night."

"Oh, my God. This is a mother's worst nightmare, what about Paula?"

TWENTY-NINE

Eden stumbled and wove as she tried to find her way back to the cabin down the snaking gravel driveway. It took every ounce of her fiber to not just lie down in the long grass and sleep. The sky, being starless and moonless, felt like a scene out of a Gothic novel. Her journey was lit by a weak light on a pole half way between the lodge and their cabin. The night was like a dark cloak that wrapped itself around her exhausted body. After stumbling several times, she found her way to the cabin porch and entered. Amazingly, she remembered to lock the frail door after closing it.

Eden attempted to slip into her pajamas, but it was too difficult as her vision grayed. She ended up climbing into her cold damp bed wearing only her underwear. How could I be drunk?, she asked. Then her disjointed thoughts rolled her into blackness. She heard the key in the lock. "Shhh," she mumbled. "Be quiet and let me sleep. I'm so tired."

The full moon shone through the dirty window with enough brightness to semi-illuminate the room. Eden felt someone standing over her small bed. "Go to bed and leave me alone until tomorrow. We'll talk in the morning."

"No, we'll talk now." The voice was slow and deep.

Eden's eyes flew open to see Jerry Anderson standing over her bed. He had already removed his soiled tan pants and his underwear. He was standing above her stark naked. She could make out his form in the dark room.

"Did I somehow doze off and drift into this nightmare?"

His eyes gleaming, he replied. "Yes, my little chicken, this is an erotic dream. I see my sleeping concoction didn't quite knock you out, like I hoped. You obviously weren't a good girl. You didn't drink all your wine. It's okay, you're groggy enough."

He lowered himself on top of her, both of her wrists were roughly caught over her head in just one of his hands.

Eden tried to think, but her mind was fuzzy. It was extremely fuzzy. She ordered herself to focus. The black void in her head threatened to obliterate her. She had back flashes of the desperate helpless feeling she had as a child. She was paralyzed both with fear and familiarity.

"Relax and give in to it. I can be anything you want me to be. I can be gentle, and I can be tender. Or, I can be brutal, it's your choice my little pet."

Her face averted from his naked body. With all the training, both with words and force, Eden's mind would not function. It was such a stark reminder of days long past.

"Do you have any idea how wonderful your sweet smelling little bodies felt against me?"

Oh, my God, she thought, what shall I do? If he would only let go of my wrists. But then what? She was drenched in icy sweat, realizing that her muscles were mush. Her purse that she dropped by the side of the bed beckoned her. Even the thought of it made her body go rigid.

"You perverted son of a bitch. If you weren't so pathetic, you'd be somewhat comical. How can you live with your filthy conscience?"

Eden's slurred words sounded as though they were coming from someone else, leaving her lips in a slow slur. Her prolific imagination began to conjure up many dark scenarios for what she would like to happen, but she couldn't seem to get her bearings.

The hatred etched in his flabby features was ugly. His voice deepened to a husky whisper. "Don't be so coy, we both know that you enjoyed it."

She began to speak, but he silenced her mouth with a sloppy wet kiss. His breath was foul, reeking of booze, cigar smoke, and rotting teeth. He momentarily removed his lips from her mouth. His hand drifted to the curve of her breast, making groans of pleasure.

"Yum, seems like you've grown some beasts since the last time we were together."

Every curve of her body was fitted to his. She now realized that somehow he had ripped off her panties.

Eden knew that even though the event seemed like slow motion, it wasn't. She would have to make her move before it was too late. The pain in her head was almost unbearable. Time was definitely not her friend.

"Don't make me work for everything. Open your legs, you uppity little bitch."

Should I just offer myself into nauseating submission?, she wondered. No. Never again I'll fight him to my death, but how am I going to draw enough strength? Her eyes had somewhat adjusted to the dark room, making his all too familiar erection visible in the moonlight. Even in her foggy state, she knew that screaming would be futile. Eden pretended to go limp as if she passed out from his drugs that he put into her wine.

In her private fog, she heard his voice go fierce. "God damn it, wake up." Calming a bit, he continued. "Maybe this is better, now I don't have to deal with your mouth or your fighting. You were always my favorite, you never screamed or cried."

Her temper mounted, and she had to struggle to keep it in check. She knew it wasn't the right time, plus, she long since gave up the idea of trying to reason with him. It was time to try something else.

He couldn't manage to penetrate Eden holding both of her wrists. Eden could feel the inside of her leg bruising. He opted to let go now that she was unconscious. She took quick advantage of her freedom.

Eden opened her hands and with one fast slash, her fingernails ripped the skin from his face.

"Oh, shit" was his sound of surprise and pain. Then she poked her knuckles into his eyes. She quickly reached down and into her purse, she retrieved her coveted revolver.

The gunshot was heard at the lodge. "Oh, my God, we need to get to Eden."

The three women ran through the still black night to the cabin. Melissa fell in her haste, but nobody even stopped or commented. They were focused on getting to the cabin as fast as possible. The door wasn't locked, and it remained slightly opened. The sight they encountered caused them to become wordless in shock.

Eden was naked and sprawled lifeless across the bed, seemingly unconscious. Jerry was bloody and had fallen in a grotesque heap onto the floor.

Melissa screamed. "Are they dead? Oh, my God, Eden are you okay? Call the ambulance. Call 911, hurry."

Nancy took Eden's cell phone out of her purse and made the call before she felt for Eden's pulse.

"Eden opened her eyes. He tried to rape the wrong little girl."

"He might bleed to death if they don't get here soon." But in spite of that announcement, Nancy made no attempt to help.

From a few feet away, Phyllis starred in shocked awe, unable to move or utter a single word. It took several seconds for Nancy to get her bearings. "Melissa, take Phyllis outside, she's going into shock."

"No, I want to stay. My days of avoidance and denial need to be over, here and now."

Eden slowly pulled herself to a sitting position, and Melissa tossed her some clothes. "Let me help you get dressed before Sheriff Cromwell gets here."

"How much damage did I do?"

"Not much." Melissa started to laugh. She laughed long and she laughed loud. Melissa's laugh was high, hysterical and uncontrollable. She laughed so hard that tears ran down her cheeks and she gasped, choking for breath. "Honey, you blew off his penis."